ESSENCE

The E.S.T. Org.

Book 1

William Fernandez

To Nicky - The inspiration for it all.

To Willy and Isa – Two stars who light up my sky every day.

To my awesome partner and wife. Thanks for all of your constant support and putting up with me. Love you tons!!
-As written by my editor and wife, although I do love you tons.

Thanks to Wayne Dyer. I didn't die with my music still in me!

Contents

PART I   **5**

CHAPTER 1 - TUMBLE   6
CHAPTER 2 - REUNION   8
CHAPTER 3 - APPETIZING   10
CHAPTER 4 - WEIRDER   18
CHAPTER 5 - STRANGER   21
CHAPTER 6 - STRESSFUL   24
CHAPTER 7 - COLLAPSE   27
CHAPTER 8 - ROCKET   31
CHAPTER 9 - HOLE   33
CHAPTER 10 - SANCTUARY   40
CHAPTER 11 - DARKNESS   46
CHAPTER 12 - SERVE   49
CHAPTER 13 - DOME   54
CHAPTER 14 - ATTACK   58
CHAPTER 15 – SMILE   63
CHAPTER 16 - HOME   66
CHAPTER 17 - BULLY   68
CHAPTER 18 - RETURN   73
CHAPTER 19 - SHOCK   75
CHAPTER 20 - FUN   81

PART II   **85**

CHAPTER 21 - AWAKENING   86
CHAPTER 22 - REVELATIONS   91
CHAPTER 23 - TOGETHER   97
CHAPTER 24 - BOOM   100
CHAPTER 25 - TOPPLE   102
CHAPTER 26 - BIRTH   107
CHAPTER 27 - INTRODUCTION   112
CHAPTER 28 - CONNECTION   116
CHAPTER 29 - ESCAPE   119
CHAPTER 30 - TIME   121
CHAPTER 31 - ESCAPE   123
CHAPTER 32 - X   127
CHAPTER 33 - FAST   129
CHAPTER 34 - AGAIN   134
CHAPTER 35 - REUNITED   138
CHAPTER 36 - SPOTTED   142

CHAPTER 37 - AWAKEN   144
CHAPTER 38 - SIX   149
CHAPTER 39 - BORED   156
CHAPTER 40 - SHOCK   159
CHAPTER 41 - DESTROY   164
CHAPTER 42 - HEALING   178
CHAPTER 43 - AGAIN   181
CHAPTER 44 - AWE   187
CHAPTER 45 - RING   192

Part I

Six months ago

Chapter 1 - Tumble

"All right Mom, I'll be right back." For about three seconds he really meant it. "Hmm … I wonder what's over there." That's all it took. "I guess I'll be right back is subjective. When is right back? Anyway …"

It was kind of a cool, dewy morning where Nicky's family had rented a cabin. It was nestled in between breathtaking mountains, a glistening river, and majestic trees that stretched beyond the human eye. He swore he saw a light out there, and he just had to walk towards it. Suddenly, he heard what sounded like an eagle. It was one of the strangest things he had ever heard … and then it happened.

Nicky saw a large opening in the ground. It was about six feet in diameter and level to the ground. Nicky got on his hands and knees to peek inside. "Cool, looks like a cave!" Suddenly, the earth gave out beneath him and he began to tumble down. He fell straight down into the cave until finally, he stopped.

"Ow! Man that hurt." He slowly got up rubbing the back of his head.

When he looked up, he could see what looked like bones. He wasn't sure if they were human or animal bones in the darkness. He was scared and thought just for a second, *"I should probably get out of here."* But Nicky wasn't really that type of kid, so further into the cave he went. What he saw amazed him. Blue, glowing artifacts that looked like Native American weapons surrounded him. He just had to touch – that's the last thing he remembered.

Chapter 2 - Reunion

Nicky woke up groggy. "Uhh … what happened? Oh no." He looked at his watch. "Mom and Dad are going to kill me!" It was almost 10:00 p.m. He ran back home. The scenery was passing him by like a blur. "*Maybe the fall made me dizzy*," he thought. "I can't think about that now; I have to get home." When he got back, he saw several police cars outside the cabin.

As he ran to the front door, he heard a scream. That was his mother and his teary-eyed father happy to see him. They hugged for what seemed like an eternity.

"What happened?" his father asked.

"I'm sorry Dad. I fell into a cave, saw some strange things, and then kind of … passed out."

"Did you hit your head?" Dad asked.

"I don't think so, but it was the coolest thing. All of these bones and these blue glowing weapons were everywhere! Well … I think they were glowing. I remember something glowing, but that's all I remember."

Nicky's parents have always known about his great imagination, but they were just so happy he was safe. After all of the police left, they hugged once more. Nicky promised to never let something like this happen again. But knowing Nicky, he will definitely get into another adventure. They all had an exhausting night and went straight to bed.

"Okay buddy, time for bed. Good night," Dad said.

Nicky replied, "Good night Mom. Good night Dad."

Chapter 3 - Appetizing

Nicky woke up feeling incredible. Maybe it was the twelve hours he was out. It was close to noon.

"Man, what a night!" He rolled out of bed, walked into the bathroom, picked up his toothbrush, and right away it snapped in his hand. "*What the? Weird,*" he thought. He stared at it for a while. Although the toothbrush broke, he was happy. He hated to brush anyway. He decided to run and hug his parents. "*Man, how'd I get so fast?*" he thought. "*I need to sleep twelve hours all the time.*"

Nicky ran to give his mother a hug. His mom was wearing a dark brown shirt and boxers that almost matched her wavy, long hair and eye color perfectly. Nicky's own hair and eyes made the family resemblance unmistakable. She was startled to see him. As he hugged her, he heard her back cracking. "Ow! Nicky, take it easy, you're going to break my back." She was puzzled.

He didn't mean to hurt her. "Sorry, Mom. I didn't mean to squeeze so tight."

Nicky then ran to his dad who was in the bathroom. The same thing happened with his dad as he was shaving his head and face. "Ouch! I'm happy to see you too, buddy," his dad exclaimed as he looked at Nicky with his deep, grey-blue eyes.

At that moment Nicky felt strange, somehow connected to the earth and the animals outside.

The family sat down at the kitchen table a few minutes later to eat an organic spinach and egg omelet. Nicky's mom was a bit of a health nut.

Nicky felt compelled to ask a question. "Dad, can we go see bears and buffalo? Can we please?"

His parents stared at him stunned.

"See bears and buffalo? You mean, you want to buy an Xbox game where you hunt bears and buffalo?" Mom questioned.

Nicky wasn't exactly the outdoorsy type. He was more of the stare at the TV connected to the Xbox for hours type. Although, he was slender at five feet five inches and 120 pounds, his parents believed that he was skinny from all the calories he exerted speaking all the time.

"No … well, I'd just like to see them. And I kind of know where they are."

"You know where they are!? How do you know where they are?" Dad asked puzzled.

"I sense them," Nicky responded.

"I wonder how hard he hit his head," Nicky's mother whispered to his dad.

"Okay Nicky, let's see if you really know where they are," his dad said obviously not believing him.

As all three of them got into the car, Nicky noticed that he could hear all of the wildlife around them so much more clearly than he ever had before. And strangely, he almost understood some of the noises. *"This is so weird,"* he thought.

"Okay Nicky, which way?" Dad asked.

Nicky's dad followed his directions. Nicky was amazed at the beauty around him; the mountain scenery is nothing like the flat lands of Florida he was used to.

Twenty minutes later, there they were, surrounded by the majestic scenery with buffalo all around them.

"How'd you know there'd be bison here?"

"I told you. I kind of sensed them."

"Really!?" Nicky's dad was even more puzzled. *"That's impossible,"* Nicky's dad thought. "Well, did you know they were hunted almost to extinction?" Gill, Nicky's dad, liked to throw in some trivia every now and then to show how smart he was.

"I know Dad. I have read a few books," explained Nicky.

Unfortunately for his dad, sometimes his trivia nuggets didn't always work out.

"Mom, Dad … you see that beautiful eagle's nest?" Nicky questioned pointing towards a large spruce tree.

"Where?" Mom asked.

But, before she could even hear the answer, Nicky had thrown open the door and was just below the eagle's nest hundreds of yards away.

When his parents finally caught up with him, his dad asked, "Did you eat your Wheaties today or something? Man, you need to start track when we get home."

Nicky knew something very strange was going on, but still all he thought to himself was, *"This is so cool!"*

In an instant, Nicky was twenty feet up in the tree.

"Nicky, get down! You'll break your neck if you fall!" his mother yelled.

"But, but …"

"Now!" she yelled back.

He thought for a second of disobeying his mother. Nicky was fourteen now, but he was still a little afraid of his mother's temper, even with the conservative glasses and standing at only five feet four inches. She was shorter than he was, but she was tough.

"Okay Mom, I just wanted to talk to them." At this point, his parents were beginning to get concerned.

"Gill, do you think he hit his head in that cave? Maybe he has a concussion," his mother questioned.

"I don't know. He is acting awfully strange. Maybe we'll take him to the doctor when we get home. But, that doesn't answer his speed or strength or how he sensed the bison? Maybe something strange did happen to him in that cave," Nicky's dad wondered.

"What do you mean strange? He just hit his head. He must be suffering from a concussion or something, and I'm worried about him," his mom responded.

"I know you are, Mara." Nicky's dad thought his mother, Mara, always had to worry about something.

"Why don't we take him to the hospital for some scans," his mother suggested.

"Don't worry so much. I doubt he even hurt his head." As Nicky's parents were lost in all of the 'what ifs', Nicky was in a stream trying to catch a fish with his bare hands.

"Hey Mom, Dad, I caught one with my bare hands!"

"Yeah, okay Nicky."

"No, really I caught one!"

"That's nice Nicky," Dad said.

"No really … look!"

Nicky turned around and lifted his arms.

"Ahhh!" his mom screamed and his dad gave him the 'what the hell look.' You know the look, the kind only a shocked father can give. Nicky was holding the large salmon in his bare hands.

"Buddy, put that back," Dad said as he shook his head. "We're going to KFC later. Salmon is not on the menu there," his dad said.

"Sure Dad." Nicky started to think, *"Maybe I could just take one bite. This is so weird but I bet it tastes like chocolate cheesecake. One bite won't hurt."* He discreetly took a huge bite. "Oh yeah! It tastes even better than chocolate cheesecake." The sight of a half bitten, bloody salmon sitting in his hands didn't bother him one bit. *"Maybe I'll just keep this to myself,"* Nicky thought.

After they all piled into the car, Nicky's dad was still curious.

"How did you do that buddy?" his dad asked puzzled.

"I don't know, I just kind of reached out and … did it."

"Huh, okay I guess. Well, did you know salmon can travel up to 3500 miles to spawn? And they can lay up to 7000 eggs?" His dad felt compelled to drop a little trivia.

"No, that's cool. But I do know that they taste delicious," Nicky responded.

"Well, let's go!" Before driving off, Nicky's mom and dad looked at each other a little dumbfounded after what they had just seen.

On the way to KFC, all Nicky could think about was salmon. "Dad? How about Red Lobster instead? They got great salmon I hear."

16

"No Nicky, I'm in the mood for chicken," his dad answered.

"Hmmm … Maybe we should get him looked at."

"Really? Now who's worried? I could just make him a salmon burger when we get home," his mom smiled and winked at his dad.

Chapter 4 - Weirder

As they were finishing up their bucket of chicken for dinner, Nicky was still pining for salmon. "We should have gone to Red Lobster instead."

"The day you pay buddy, we'll go wherever you want," his dad said smirking.

After they finished eating, Nicky's mom was ready for grocery shopping. "Ready guys? I need to get to the market."

As they walked towards the car, Nicky's dad thought aloud, "I'm sure the day can't get any weirder ... can it?"

When they got back to the cabin from grocery shopping, Dad had to ask Nicky something that was gnawing at him. "So, Nicky, could you show me where this cave is?"

"Sure Dad, let's go!" Nicky said.

"Okay Nicky, but at a human speed this time. I'm not a gazelle."

Nicky laughed, "Sure." And off they went.

It was a two mile hike through the mountainous forest. Dad really felt it. Nicky was ready for a few marathons. "Come on Dad! Hurry up! I can't go any slower!"

"Okay, okay, just hold on," Nicky's dad said to him. "*Man this kid has gotten fast,*" his dad thought.

At the exact same time Nicky thought, "*Man, he's slow.*"

"It's just over there." Nicky pointed to a nearby clearing.

Deep in the woods they saw it. It resembled a crop circle in the middle of the forest.

"Whoa, it wasn't like this before, I swear. There were trees here. And the cave was right there," Nicky pointed towards the ground.

Nicky started to feel strange again, like he was somehow connected to whatever or whomever was just there. As Dad approached the center of the circle, he noticed deep gashes in the trees surrounding the circle.

"You see those?" Dad asked.

"Yeah, they weren't there before," Nicky replied.

"Strange … So, where did you fall?"

"The opening was right here in the middle of the circle. There was an opening right here," Nicky said perplexed.

Just then, as he stood in the center of the circle, Nicky collapsed.

"Nicky? Nicky?" His dad checked for breathing. He was still breathing, so his dad quickly picked him up and started the long journey back to the cabin.

Almost twenty minutes later, he finally got close enough to the cabin and yelled out to Nicky's mom, "Mara! Call 911!"

"What happened?"

"He just passed out, but he's still breathing. Hurry!"

Chapter 5 - Stranger

Nicky woke up in the hospital a few hours later. He opened his eyes and saw his father. "Dad? Why am I here? What happened?"

"The doctors aren't sure buddy." His parents were just relieved that he was awake. "When you stood in the center of the circle, you just passed out, but there are no internal injuries and all of the brain scans were normal. Maybe you're just exhausted."

"Oh, okay ... Hey Dad?"

"Yeah"

"Could I have a salmon burger?"

"Anything you want, Monkey." That was his dad's nickname for Nicky. His parents laughed.

"He is a very focused kid," his mom told his dad.

About a half hour later, Nicky's mother told the doctors about his disappearance. After learning about the particulars, the doctors asked Nicky's parents if they could observe him for a few more days. Nicky's parents agreed.

"You know buddy, we spoke to the doctors and they think you should stay here for a couple of days," Dad informed him.

"What? Why? I feel fine."

"I know. They just want to make sure that you're okay."

"Man … but … but …"

"Sorry, buddy. No buts. We want to make sure that you're okay. I promise salmon for breakfast, lunch, and dinner if you want."

"Fine … I guess that doesn't sound so bad."

Two days passed. His mom and dad were at his side every minute, only leaving to eat or take a short break. Nicky was growing restless watching television all day. More tests, more doctors, and again all the tests came back normal.

Finally they got the good news. "We can't find any abnormalities. You can take him home now. If there are any changes in his condition, bring him back immediately," one of the doctors explained as he signed the discharge papers.

Nicky overheard the doctor. "Oh Yeah!!" Nicky jumped out of bed. "Let's go!"

"Okay Nicky, let's go back to the cabin."

When they got back to the cabin, Dad shared with his mother what happened the night Nicky collapsed. "You know it was the strangest thing."

"What's that?" Nicky's mom asked.

"As soon as he stepped in the center of the circle, I felt a strong breeze and Nicky just collapsed. It was the same spot he said he fell through an opening."

"Really?"

"And the way he's been behaving … I don't know. Something strange is going on."

"Hey, I heard that!" Nicky said from across the hall.

"You see? And we're whispering," his dad continued.

"You know what? Tomorrow is our last day. Let's just have some fun," Mom said.

"You're right. And hey, it couldn't get any strang …"

"Just shut up," his mom interrupted. They both laughed.

Chapter 6 - Stressful

The final morning of their vacation started early. When Nicky came to the table, Dad said, "What a week, huh buddy?"

"Yeah, it's been pretty amazing."

They all sat down for breakfast. Mom had made a special salmon omelet.

As Nicky's dad took a bite of the omelet, he said, "I'm learning to like these things."

"Mmm, that was delicious. I know what we should do," Nicky announced.

"Okay, what's that?" Mom questioned.

"Can we go to Mount McKinley?" Nicky asked.

"Sure. Sounds like fun to me," his dad responded.

Mount McKinley was the largest mountain in the area.

After a twisting car ride through the scenic mountains, they arrived about an hour later.

When they started their hike, Nicky made sure to slow way down for his parents. They all stopped about half way up the mountain amazed at what they saw. An eagle swooped down about five feet away from Nicky. He felt a strong connection with the eagle. As the bird approached Nicky, his dad yelled, "Careful!"

"It's okay, Dad. Don't worry. He won't hurt me." Nicky sat down and the eagle approached and landed. They sat together for a few minutes and then the eagle flew off.

"Holy crap," Dad exclaimed. "Mara, you remember the horse whisperer?"

"Yeah."

"I think Nicky's better."

Nicky smiled, "He just wanted to say hello to a friend."

"When we get back home, maybe we should just keep this to ourselves. Okay Nicky?"

"Sure Dad, don't worry."

They continued their hike through the breathtaking trail that was surrounded by rivers, spruce trees, and green landscapes. Further up the mountain, Nicky asked, "Dad, can we come back next year?"

"I'll think about it. You know Nicky, I think a vacation in the Middle East would be less stressful than these woods."

Chapter 7 - Collapse

After a few days and a long, uneventful drive, the Hernandez family finally arrived home.

They began to unload the ten pieces of luggage so they could relax after the long drive.

"I think we could classify that as the strangest vacation ever," Nicky's dad told his mom. Mom laughed.

"Mom, when do I start school?"

"In a little over a week," Mom answered.

"Aww, Maybe I could have a few more weeks off. You know I am seriously injured."

"Sorry, Nicky. Nice try," his dad said.

As they finished unloading the last of the large, black generic luggage that abounds in every Target store, Nicky could see a strange light peering through the clouds. Nicky instinctively knew it was meant for him. "*I don't want to scare Mom and Dad. I'll just keep this to myself*," he thought.

The next day, Sue and Becky, Nicky's friends from the neighborhood, were knocking on his door at 9:00 a.m.

Nicky didn't have many friends, only Becky and Sue. But as Dad always said, 'It's better to have a couple of good friends than a hundred bad ones.'

Sue and Becky's parents weren't really the most attentive or caring people. All summer long the kids came over, almost daily, and always early in the morning. They spent so much time there, Nicky's parents called Sue and Becky their 'adopted kids.'

"Nicky!" Sue screamed as Nicky opened the door. Sue was the older of the sisters. She was around Nicky's age and a year older than Becky. She was tall at five feet five inches, with long blond hair and slender. She always wore tank tops and shorts that were two sizes too small.

And Becky, well, she was short, with rarely washed mousey brown hair, and a little chubby. She always wore clothes that looked two sizes too big. They couldn't look more opposite.

Nicky's mom and dad were still sleeping, exhausted from the long drive home.

"So how was the trip?" Sue asked.

Nicky almost spilled the beans about what happened. "I fell and the most amazing … well I mean I hit my head and went to the hospital, but besides that, not much really."

"Really? I'm glad you're okay. I thought you would have all kinds of stories for us. Well, my brother is out of jail and back with us. He promised not to set fires and my mom really believes him this time. Oh and remember Karen? Well, her parents divorced and her dad fled the country. Oh, and Joe from three blocks down, well he got a job, but was fired after crashing a company car in to someone's living room. Anyway, let's play some ball!" Sue was a very quick talker and rarely stayed on a single subject for too long. She was known as the neighborhood gossip.

"Okay, let me ask my mom and dad." But as Nicky turned around to go ask his parents if they could play basketball, he felt a sharp pain in his head. He cried out loudly, "Oww!"

Nicky's scream woke up his parents. They ran to him. "What is it?" his dad asked obviously shaken.

"I don't know, Dad. I just saw a light and felt a sharp pain in my head."

"How do you feel now?" Mom asked concerned.

"I'm okay. I don't feel any pain."

"Okay, just remember Nicky, all the tests came back fine," Dad tried to reassure Nicky.

"I know … I just want to go hang out."

Out the door the three of them went.

"I don't know what more we can do. I just want to help him but I don't know how," Dad said.

"All we can do is just trust that he'll be fine," Mom said.

Chapter 8 - Rocket

"Are you okay?" Becky asked Nicky just outside his house.

It was a sunny, hot and humid South Florida morning. They lived in a typical middle class neighborhood that was built in the 1990's. A place where the single story stucco houses were too close, but the lawns were green and manicured. All of the flower beds were lined with the Homeowner's Association compliant red mulch.

"I'm fine. I told you I bumped my head. Really, it's fine."

"Okay. So, you want to race there?" Becky asked.

"Okay." Nicky didn't really think about his new found speed and forgot he ran like a shuttle taking off now. He was already at the half-acre neighborhood park, while the girls were still far behind. When they finally arrived, they looked at Nicky shocked.

"How did you do that?" Sue asked.

"*Oh no*," he thought. Then he said to Becky and Sue, "Well … it's just … these new skate shoes."

"Oh really?" Sue said scratching her head. "Well those shoes are amazing."

"Yeah, we could barely see you," Becky said.

"Ha-ha, yeah they're really cool, electric powered for extra speed. Anyway, let's play." Nicky wanted to quickly change the subject. They played basketball in the hot sun for hours. Nicky made sure to hide his new 'abilities' even though he still needed to win.

Chapter 9 - Hole

Nicky was still dreaming when his dad's voice woke him up. "Good morning Monkey, first day of school, buddy. Eighth grade already! You are getting so old."

Groggily Nicky replied, "Okay ... I'm up Dad."

"Now remember, don't tell anyone what happened or let them know about your new ... skills."

"Okay, okay Dad, don't worry. Can I just sleep a little longer?"

"No! Get up; don't make your mother late."

He got on his favorite red shorts that probably should have been thrown away six months ago and a solid black top. Nicky was sad, there was no salmon today, just a bowl of cereal.

Nicky's mom drove him to his first day of school. She was a sixth grade math teacher at the school. A lot of the other kids thought Nicky got preferential treatment for being a teacher's kid. If the kids only knew how scared the principal was of the parents. She would always cave to the parent's demands.

On his way out of their once tan, large SUV that should have been traded in years ago, Mom blurted out to Nicky loudly, "Love you!"

"Not so loud Mom, I'm a studly eighth grader now."

"Oh really? Well, since you're so old and studly now, how about you get a job and help with the bills at home?" Nicky smiled and shut the door.

Nicky's first day of school had to include Max the bully. At almost five feet seven inches already, he was a thick 150 pounds. Max had dark brown hair that was shaved on the sides with a curly Mohawk on top. He had eyes that Nicky described as black and beady. Before he could reach his first class he heard the voice that had tormented him for so long.

"Hey dummy!" Max 'lovingly' yelled out to Nicky.

They were close to the bathrooms in a secluded spot of the school. Max figured if he hurt Nicky, no one would see or hear them.

"Just stay away from me." Nicky felt differently than he had in the past. He didn't fear Max like he had for the last couple of years. When Max approached Nicky from behind to give him his regular wedgie, Nicky felt a burst of anger. As he turned his head

34

towards Max, he let out what sounded like a loud roar. It knocked Max on his butt. Luckily it wasn't a direct hit, only a glancing blow. It could have been much worse.

Max was scared and so was Nicky. Nicky had already disobeyed his father. Max ran screaming and crying down the hall as kids and faculty ran into the hallway to see what had happened. Nicky ran and hid in the bathroom.

"What was that?" another boy in the bathroom asked Nicky.

Nicky played it off. "I don't know."

He hurried back to his first class, which was his least favorite subject, English. The rest of the day was uneventful.

As the final bell rang for the day, all Nicky wanted to do was to go home, have another salmon omelet, and forget the day. He couldn't shake the incident with Max. As cool as Nicky thought roaring like an animal and knocking someone down was, Nicky felt scared and confused, and he wanted answers. *"What happened to me in that cave?"* He thought.

Nicky's dad was waiting for him in the car loop in their four door 'sexy sedan,' as his dad referred to it. The 2009 Pontiac G8 was highly customized, and Nicky's dad felt an uncomfortable affection towards it. "What's up, buddy? Get in! I got something special for you."

As they drove away, Nicky noticed the same light in the sky that had tormented him a few days ago.

"*I'm guessing only I can see it*," he thought to himself. "So where are we going?" he asked his dad.

"Well, since you love fish so much now, we're going fishing."

"Cool," Nicky said.

"Take a look." Nicky's dad pointed to the back seat.

Nicky turned around to take a look "Cool." Two new shiny, red fishing rods were laying in the back seat.

They drove to a pier on a lake five miles away from school. Nicky wanted to catch fish with his bare hands again, but he thought to himself, "*That may look a little weird.*" As they cast out, Nicky felt happy that he was fishing with his dad, but still uneasy about the strange light following them. "Dad, can I tell you something?"

"Sure Monkey, what's up?"

"I think we're being followed."

"Followed? By who?" Dad asked.

"I don't know. It's just a strange light in the sky."

At this point Nicky's dad knew it wasn't just his imagination, and was taking Nicky's concerns seriously.

"Do you see it now?"

"No, but they're close. They were just following us. My guess is, soon we'll find out who they are," Nicky stated with concern in his voice.

That night Nicky had a nightmare. It was full of wild North American animals chasing him relentlessly, while Native Americans were watching and following him from a distance. The Native Americans yelled at him until he woke up sweaty and screaming.

Nicky's mom ran to his room. "Honey, are you okay?" Mom asked worried.

"Yeah, I'm fine Mom, just a nightmare."

"What about, dear?"

"It was nothing, Mom." Nicky didn't want his mother to worry any more than she has.

"Okay. I love you." She kissed his forehead, "Good night."

Dad was still out cold. A bomb could go off and his dad could sleep through it.

As Nicky laid back down, he noticed a blue tinted light shining dimly behind the closed blinds. "Oh no, they're here."

Suddenly, the light disappeared. He looked through the window and saw a tall, dark figure. He tried to scream but only a powerful roar came out of him, just like in school. The roar made the window explode towards the backyard along with the dark figure. His dad and mom ran in moments later.

"I'm sorry. I'm sorry. There was someone out there."

They couldn't believe their eyes. Dad checked the back yard. "There's no one here."

The window was gone and pieces of the wall could be seen sitting outside. Some pieces of glass and wall were more than twenty feet away. Neighbors started to gather in front of the house.

Dad stepped outside to reassure them. "It's okay. It was just a tree that fell in the backyard. It's fine." Dad didn't like lying, but he had to protect Nicky.

Now Nicky and his parents were sure something or someone was after Nicky, and his new abilities had something to do with it.

"Don't worry about it, Nicky." Dad placed a flattened cardboard box over the hole and sealed it with duct tape. "That should be fine until we get it fixed. So, how did you do this?"

"Not sure Dad. I was angry and scared and a noise like a roar came out of me. And well ... it made whoever was out there go flying backwards."

"What?!" his mom said startled.

"Amazing ... that is pretty cool. You know sonic weapons are said to be in use by our own government right now," his dad quipped.

"Gill, please, this is serious," his mom said angrily.

"Hey, I wish I could do that," his dad said back to his mom. Nicky smiled. "Okay buddy, why don't you sleep on the couch tonight?"

Chapter 10 - Sanctuary

"Good morning, Nicky." His dad said on another sunny Saturday morning.

"Morning Mom, morning Dad," Nicky said just waking up from the living room couch, his hair sticking straight up.

"So how was the couch?" asked Mom.

"It was okay I guess. And I'm sorry about the wall."

"Don't sweat it. Just think of our new hole as a cheap skylight, only … on the wall." Dad was trying to make Nicky laugh and forget about last night.

But Nicky was still shaken and his dad could see it. He put his arm around him.

"I don't know what's after you Monkey, but I think whatever it is, you can stop them. You have some pretty amazing abilities now. Just remember how powerful you are and have always been. Maybe you don't believe it now son, but some day you will."

Nicky looked up and smiled at his father.

His dad tried to change the subject. "I know you have a special connection with animals. Why don't we go to the animal sanctuary? Maybe you can communicate with some of the animals there."

"Sure, sounds good to me," Nicky replied.

After eating breakfast, a salmon omelet of course, Nicky and his dad jumped into the car and headed north. This drive was very different from the picturesque mountain roads their vacation provided. It was on a flat highway hugged by concrete barriers; the monotony was only broken up by the sporadic graffiti and aggressive drivers. They arrived at the sanctuary about forty minutes later, parking in the gravel lot next to the main building.

The Johnson Animal Sanctuary was a beautiful facility with hundreds of acres. Hundreds of animals are rehabilitated to be released into the wild. For some of the animals who can no longer take care of themselves, it became a permanent home.

The entrance was an unspectacular chain link fence with an old faded sign that said, "Entrance." Behind the fence was a wondrous facility that got by on donations and a deep love for the animals.

Nicky was immediately drawn to an old grizzly bear in a large enclosure. The onlookers were amazed as the bear hobbled right up to the fence where Nicky stood. Nicky sat, and remarkably without saying a word, communicated with the bear just feet away. The bear told him all about his life and how a trap had permanently injured him and brought him to the sanctuary. It wasn't really a conversation like two people would normally have; it was telepathic and without words. Still the ideas and images came across to Nicky. He felt a deep connection with the bear. A tear trickled down Nicky's face. He felt badly for this beautiful bear; this bear who once roamed freely. But Nicky found some solace knowing this amazing place would always take care of him.

As the crowd grew, a volunteer appeared and was shocked by what he saw. It looked like the two of them were sitting and having a silent conversation. "Is that your son?" asked the volunteer.

"Oh, yeah, he really loves animals. He's like the bear whisperer."

"Well, I've never seen Blue behave this way."

"Nicky just kind of has a way with animals. It almost seems like they talk to him," Nicky's dad laughed nervously.

42

"Amazing! Do you mind if he meets Mr. Johnson?" asked the volunteer.

"Really? Oh wow!" Dad exclaimed. "Nicky?"

"Yeah Dad?"

"Would you like to meet the owner of the sanctuary?" Dad asked.

"Well, yeah!"

The volunteer got on his radio and in two minutes a short, bulky, jovial guy showed up. He was balding and wearing what all the other employees wore, jeans and a long sleeved button down khaki shirt with the sanctuary logo.

"Mr. Johnson, this is Gill and his son Nicky," the volunteer introduced them.

"Nice to meet you!" Mr. Johnson went on to say, "They tell me Blue really likes you. I've never seen Blue get that close to the fence, and he's been here almost five years."

"Well, it's pretty amazing what Nicky can do with animals," Dad said.

"Can I give you two a personal tour?" Mr. Johnson asked.

Nicky just smiled.

"Absolutely!" Dad exclaimed.

They saw many different types of animals from raccoons to snakes and even a mountain lion. The animals didn't react quite the same way as Blue did. But then Mr. Johnson took them to see Old Chuck.

"Here is our bald eagle rehab area." As Mr. Johnson explained how they care for the eagles, Old Chuck flew and landed right next to Nicky. And again, Nicky sat down and was able to communicate telepathically. Mr. Johnson was stunned by what he saw. The eagle looked like he was nodding in agreement as Nicky and Old Chuck had what seemed like a conversation. This went on for about ten minutes.

"Just amazing," Mr. Johnson said.

"I know. He has a special connection with some animals," Dad explained.

"Do you think Nicky would like to volunteer?" Mr. Johnson asked.

"I'm sure he'd like that," but in the back of Nicky's father's mind, all he could think of was whomever or whatever was after his son.

44

At the end of the tour, Nicky's dad thanked Mr. Johnson.

"Come back anytime, and remember Nicky, we'd love to have you when you're ready."

"Thanks Mr. Johnson, I'm sure I'll be back."

As they got to the car, Nicky told his dad, "That was awesome! When can we come back?"

"Soon, Nicky," his dad said with concern in his voice. "I'm just afraid of anyone finding out about your new abilities. We have to keep this a secret, you know?"

"Yeah, I guess you're right, Dad. It was amazing. You know they told me all about what they went through. The bear had cubs and lived in a beautiful forest before he was injured. And the eagle loved to hunt fish just like me. He remembered a loud boom and pain in his wing. I tried to explain what a gun was to him."

"That's pretty amazing Nicky. We'll tell Mom all about it when we get home. And remember ..."

"I know," Nicky interrupted, "Keep it to ourselves."

Chapter 11 - Darkness

"Morning, Monkey!" Nicky's room was now boarded up. Mondays were not Nicky's favorite day.

"School time … oh yeah … oh yeah," his dad tried to sing a catchy tune.

And like every Monday, Nicky replied groggily, "Thanks. I know, Dad."

On the way to school Nicky saw the light again, but this time he thought to himself, *"Come on! I'm ready! Bring it on!"*

During lunch, Nicky, Sue, and Becky got caught up on what they did over the weekend.

"Well, we went to Johnson Animal Sanctuary, and I got a private tour from Mr. Johnson."

"Really?" Sue said surprised. "How?"

"Oh. Well, I'm sure my dad paid extra for that." Somehow Nicky had become a master at lying, definitely another one of his gifts. They gossiped for a while, then went back to class for an uneventful day.

46

Although Nicky's mom was a teacher at the school, she could no longer take Nicky home with her. Nicky's dad was forced to pick him up every day. They changed the rules last year after some parents complained to the principal. Teachers used to be able to keep their own kids in their classrooms for forty-five minutes afterschool and avoid paying aftercare. And as always, the scared principal caved to those parents. So, his dad had to leave work at 2:00 p.m. every day and give up his lunch break to pick up Nicky. *"They don't seem to care when teachers are forced to pay for their kid's school supplies!"* Nicky's dad angrily thought to himself. He strained every day to smile at the parents who forced the rule change.

Outwardly Nicky's dad said, "Oh, hi Angie. Hey, hi there Sal." But inwardly he thought, *"Hi, idiot; hey there moron."* Nicky's dad even forced a halfway believable smile that day.

After the bell, Nicky walked up to the car and his dad greeted him. "Hey Monkey, how was your day?"

"Pretty good," he answered after getting into the car.

A few minutes later, on the routine drive home, a tire blew. As his dad changed the tire, quietly whispering expletives to himself, Nicky saw the light again. Almost simultaneously in the rear view mirror, he noticed a dark van approaching at a high rate of speed. It slammed on its brakes and stopped right next to them. It all happened so fast. Five men, a Taser and then … darkness.

Chapter 12 - Serve

Nicky woke up strapped to a metal bed. It was a cold, white room. One wall looked like a mirror. Even the floor and ceiling were a glossy white. There was nothing else in the room but the metal bed and a few recessed lights in the ceiling.

Nicky didn't know what to think. Maybe he was happy; he could finally meet who was following him all this time. "*Where am I?*" he thought. "I want out!" he yelled.

At that moment he easily broke free from the leather straps that were restraining him.

"Please, Nicholas." One of the mirrors opened like a door. A man walked in to the room. "Please calm down. You are in no danger here."

"I don't care, I want to go home now!" Nicky demanded.

"Yes, soon. We just need to observe you." The stranger in dark blue coveralls said with his hands up, visibly nervous as if he knew about Nicky's new abilities.

"What? Why?!" yelled Nicky.

"Well, you have been through a delicate procedure."

"Procedure? What do you mean procedure?"

"It is complicated," said the man. He was wearing a white lab coat.

"I want to see my family."

"You will. As soon as we are done with our assessments, you may go."

"Where is my father?" Nicky demanded.

"He is fine; he is back at home. I am sorry, but we assumed you would not come voluntarily and with these … well, new abilities you now possess. It may have been dangerous for all involved." The man then asked gently, "Please, come with me Nicholas."

Nicky was angry and scared, but now he felt more confident he could handle any situation. And he wanted answers.

As they walked down a long white hallway, Nicky noticed something strange. All of the men they passed looked incredibly similar. All of them had greasy black hair, pale skin, and intense blue eyes. All were about six feet tall. It was as if they were all cousins from the same strange family. Those who weren't in lab coats wore identical, dark blue coveralls.

At the end of the corridor was a white door with a sign that read, "Director." Through the door sat a long white table. It was a glossy, white table with eight white, shiny chairs sitting neatly in front. Even the walls and floor looked like white lacquer.

Another pale, black haired, blue eyed man in a white lab coat was sitting behind the desk. Only facial features dissimilar to the others was his broad face and nose. "Please come in, Nicholas. I am Mr. Macken. I am sorry we had to acquire you in such a manner, but what has merged with you could be very powerful and dangerous indeed."

"Merged! What do you mean merged?" Nicky paused then shouted angrily before Mr. Macken could speak. "You know what, I don't care. I just want to go home now!"

"Oh yes, absolutely, but tell me Nicholas, do you want to hurt your parents?"

"No. Of course not!"

"Well, you see the merging could cause you to lose control and conceivably, even kill you parents. The way your anger is manifesting right now is not how you typically behave. You want to hurt me do you not? That same rage could be visited upon them."

51

"I would never hurt my parents and what is this merging you keep talking about?" Nicky asked.

"You would not hurt them consciously Nicholas, but we have seen it before. You must be taught how to control what is inside you now. You see Nicholas we have chosen you to merge with specific animals. We are a classified government agency. We are equipped with advanced scientific teams that have developed the ability to merge animals with humans. You are one of the lucky few who now possess incredible abilities beyond that of any human."

"Wait, so you're turning me into an animal?"

"No Nicholas, you have simply been enhanced with certain characteristics of select animals we have chosen. So you see, we had no choice but to bring you here to our training facility so you may be trained to eventually serve your country."

"So you forced me to 'merge' with animals and then want to force me to work for you?"

"Nicholas, your country has chosen you and you must answer the call. Now please be aware your parents are back home and secure. They have been informed of the particulars and are proud you have been chosen to serve."

"Why have I been asked to serve?"

"I am sorry Nicholas. I am afraid the circumstances cannot be revealed at the moment. We are in great danger."

"Fine. But tell me, when can I see my parents?" Nicky asked. Nicky began to calm down.

"Very soon, just a few more days and you may return to your home. Now, let us get to work."

Chapter 13 - Dome

As Nicky walked with Mr. Macken and two more pale men, he wondered if his family was okay.

They entered a large dome. It reminded Nicky of a football stadium, but it was all steel grey. Nicky looked up in awe. "*Man this place is huge,*" he thought.

"This is our Creation Room. We can create matter. Not exactly real, but an approximation." With one word from Mr. Macken, "Forest," the dome was transformed.

"Now Nicky, do you see that tree? Could you jump up there, on that branch?"

"All the way up there … no."

It was about twelve feet high.

"Go ahead, just try."

"Sure," Nicky replied. Thinking to himself, "*What is this idiot on?*" Nicky leapt. Not knowing what he was now capable of, he jumped over the branch by about eight feet and came crashing down.

"Wonderful Nicholas!" Mr. Macken exclaimed, without showing any concern if Nicky was injured or not.

Luckily, Nicky just brushed himself off. He stood amazed for a few seconds at what he had just done, and that he was okay after such a fall.

"How did I do that? Is the gravity lower in here or something?" Nicky asked.

"The merge has altered your physiology."

"What do you mean?" Nicky was confused.

"Well, let us just say it has impacted your body in special ways."

"Cool. What else can I do?"

"That is why we are here Nicholas. Now, do you see that deer in the distance?" Mr. Macken said pointing to a wooded area.

"Yeah."

"Could you bring him here as quickly as possible?"

"But he's so far away, and how am I going to pick him up!"

"Just attempt it." Mr. Macken told him sternly.

Nicky sprinted through the forest. The deer did not even have time to react. Nicky was back in seconds holding the 300 pound male deer with impressive six point antlers in his arms. "Holy crap, this is Superman strong!"

"Excellent, Nicholas." The deer disappeared from Nicky's arms.

"Now Nicholas, please focus. Close your eyes and point towards any sound you hear." Nicky closed his eyes and pointed directly in front of himself, then to his right and finally towards his back.

"Good. Now open your eyes. What do you see behind you?" Mr. Macken pointed towards the sound.

"Well, I see a humming bird."

"Good. That's about a mile away. That's what you heard. Well, that should be all for today."

"Great, I'm as hungry as a bear." Nicky's stomach was growling. "Can I eat yet?"

"Of course, oh I almost forgot. One quick question before we finish up for the day. If I said tash-ay-ay, nah-kee, kah-yay, tin-yay asht-lay, what does that mean?" Mr. Macken asked.

"Well you said one, two, three, four, five. But I don't know how I understood you," Nicky said puzzled.

"You will, in time Nicholas. Now, let us get you some food. What would you like to eat?"

"Fish of course."

"I can arrange that."

Chapter 14 - Attack

Nicky was escorted back to his room for lunch. They created an exact replica of his room back home. It was a fifteen feet by fifteen feet cobalt blue room with two windows and a few inappropriate posters, which his mother was trying hard to accept as Nicky was getting older. The old oak wood furniture Nicky hated was there too. *"How did they know what my room looks like, and did they have to replicate the butt ugly furniture?"* he wondered. Just like home, there was a closet full of his favorite comic books, like X-Men, Wolverine, Batman, and The Punisher. He spent the rest of the day reading them.

When he finally got bored of reading, Nicky thought, *"I miss my family. Maybe if I do everything they ask, they'll let me go home soon. Night Mom and Dad, wherever you are."* He then turned off the light and went to sleep.

It was the start of day two.

"Good morning, Nicholas."

"Great, another random pasty dude," Nicky thought.

"Good morning," Nicky replied.

"Well, Mr. Macken is waiting in the Creation Room. Are you ready to go or would you like to eat something first?" the man asked.

"No thanks. Let's get this over with," Nicky replied. They headed to the Creation Room.

"Good morning Nicholas. We have some excellent assessments for you today," Mr. Macken informed Nicky.

Nicky was not excited. He could only think of home.

"As you now know, you are linked to certain animals in extraordinary ways. Their essence has enhanced you."

"What is their 'essence'?"

"All in due time. Now please, do you see that large hill over there?" Instantly, a hill was created within a picturesque green valley. Nicky nodded. "Climb it and jump from the top, and as you fall, imagine yourself growing wings and flying."

"Jump! So you mean I can fly?" Nicky asked in amazement.

"Well Nicholas, let us just complete our assessments. Now please go ahead."

Nicky was at the thirty foot high peak within seconds.

"Okay Nicholas on three. One, two, three."

Nicky jumped. He imagined an eagle flying gracefully in the warm, beautiful, clear skies. And then … like a lead rock he came crashing straight down into a stream at the bottom of the hill.

"Well, that did not go as we had anticipated, " Mr. Macken quietly muttered to himself, again showing no concern for Nicky's well-being.

"What happened!?" Nicky yelled out after wiping the water from his face and making sure he was still in one piece.

"You see Nicholas, these assessments are being performed to see how your merges will manifest. We do not know how your body will react."

"Ah, man … I thought I could fly."

"Well that is disappointing. Nevertheless we must continue with our assessments," Mr. Macken said.

Mr. Macken took Nicky to an area where several weapons had been laid out. "Here are some weapons I would like you to try out."

In front of Nicky laid a bow and arrow, a war club, and a tomahawk.

"Cool!" Nicky was very excited.

"First let us try the bow and arrow." Nicky picked up the large forty-four inch bow made of cedar wood and buffalo sinew. The primitive arrow had an obsidian rock tip. It appeared to be over a hundred years old. "Now gently pull back and aim at that bird. Do not worry, it is not real. Now go ahead."

Nicky shot and hit the small bird over 150 yards away.

"Well done. Now, this is a war club." It looked like a big, wooden club with a leather-wrapped handle curved at the top. It had a solid wood ball almost the size of a softball at the apex. "You will be attacked by several men. Remember they are not real, they are mere simulations so do not be afraid. You will be aiming for the attackers' heads. They will simply disappear once struck. Do you understand?"

"Okay, but can they hurt me?"

"In theory, yes, but they are programmed to only try to immobilize you, not hurt you."

Mr. Macken left to observe from a safe distance. Three men in military uniforms materialized and began to attack Nicky.

The first attacker came from behind; Nicky could hear his footsteps. Nicky hesitated, but remembered that they weren't real.

He quickly swung around and hit the attacker in the head. The uniformed man disappeared.

Nicky's heart was pounding. Suddenly, the last two remaining attackers who were carrying knives ran at Nicky. Nicky ducked as one of the attackers slashed at his head. Nicky swept the attacker's legs, clubbing his head before he could even hit the floor. He disappeared. Instinctively Nicky leapt and did a back flip over the second attacker. He quickly clubbed his head. The final attacker also disappeared.

Nicky didn't know or care how he did it, but he felt excited. "This is so cool!" But suddenly another soldier with a much more powerful weapon, a machine gun, appeared!

Chapter 15 – Smile

"STOP!" And just like a DVR, the attacker froze. "Can that gun hurt me?" Nicky yelled.

Mr. Macken could be heard over a speaker. "Do not worry. The bullets cannot kill you. It may cause a mild sensation, but that is all. They are emulating a harmless pliable material."

"Okay I guess, as long as it can't hurt me." The simulation continued. The attacker fired. Nicky could hear and see the bullets as if they were in slow motion. He ran towards the attacker avoiding every bullet. Hundreds of them came at him at once. Just before reaching his attacker, Nicky roared pushing bullets out of their trajectory. Eventually, a quick strike stopped the attacker.

"Exceptional," Mr. Macken could be heard over a speaker. "Now behind you is the final weapon, a tomahawk."

Nicky thought it was beautiful and by far his favorite weapon of the three. The stone axe head sat on top of a wooden handle. It was very ornate and beautifully engraved with two feathers tied to it with a leather strap.

"A herd of buffalo will charge at you. Your task is to avoid being trampled and neutralize the buffalo with the number seven painted on his back."

"But how can I see a number painted on a buffalo's back?" Nicky asked.

"Good luck, Nicholas."

Suddenly a rumble like a passing train began to shake the ground. There was a herd of buffalo stampeding towards Nicky. Just like the bullets had before, the buffalo seemed to move in slow motion. There were thousands. Nicky stood without fear as the buffalo approached. He closed his eyes. When the buffalo were just feet away, Nicky raised his arms in a defensive position. A buffalo ran right into him. It was as if the buffalo hit a steel wall. The first buffalo's neck broke just before it collapsed and disappeared. Most of the buffalo that hit Nicky's immovable body met the same fate.

Nicky then leapt. He jumped much higher than he thought he could, and at that height he could see the entire herd. He observed many buffalo with numbers painted on their backs. Although within seconds, he recognized the buffalo with the large red number seven. It was to his left at about 10:00 o'clock. He came crashing to the ground. Immediately he jumped on a buffalo's back and then another and another until he found the number seven buffalo. With a quick strike to the head with the tomahawk, the buffalo simply disappeared, as they all did.

Mr. Macken walked back into the dome. "Marvelous! You have exceeded our expectations, Nicholas."

"Thank you," Nicky stated. "Does this mean I can go home now?"

"Of course ... of course, Nicholas. Your family is at home waiting."

Nicky didn't trust Mr. Macken, but he was hoping he could ... at least this time.

"Now, let us get you home," Mr. Macken said with what seemed like a strained smile. Nicky was surprised that Mr. Macken was forcing himself to be nice.

"Okay, so right now?"

"Certainly, go get your things, but remember we will be in contact."

Chapter 16 - Home

Nicky was so excited when he finally arrived home. Two more pasty guys, as Nicky referred to them, drove away in a dark Prius. Nicky was groggy; he had been gassed and knocked unconscious to protect the facility's location.

Nicky was standing at his front door. *"Finally, I'm free!"* he thought.

He knocked at the door with a big smile on his face. As the door opened, Nicky's dad appeared.

"Dad!" shouted Nicky.

"Nicholas is home, Mara!" his dad yelled out as they hugged. His mom wasn't far behind.

After they hugged, Nicky wanted to tell his parents everything. They sat in the living room. He told them all about his assessments and how he didn't trust those "strange looking guys."

"Do not worry, Nicholas. They explained everything to us and they are good people. They told us how you were chosen and then enhanced to help the country. You should feel privileged."

"Really, you think so?" Nicky asked his dad.

"Absolutely. Trust me, they are only interested in helping you reach your potential, and eventually helping your country," Nicky's dad told him.

"Okay Dad, if you think so."

"They will be back for more tests, but I want you to go with them and trust them. Okay?"

"If I have to, I guess."

"Do not worry. They will make your fantastic abilities even greater. Is that not good news?"

"Yeah, I guess that would be cool," Nicky responded.

"I know you will be happy, Nicholas. Now what would you like to do?"

"Sleep! And in my own bed, not some stupid replica."

Chapter 17 - Bully

"Nicholas! Your friends Sue and Becky are here!" his mom yelled. It was too early for Nicky at 10:00 a.m. on a weekend. He just wanted to sleep.

Sue and Becky came running into Nicky's room. "Where have you been?" Sue asked.

"Oh … me," He yawned. He didn't know how to respond, but he was a masterful liar. "I was with my cousins … they live just south of us."

"Oh, really? Did you have fun?"

"It was okay."

"Okay … well … you wanna go play basketball?" asked Becky.

"Nah … my cousins are really into sports. All we did was play ball all day. I'm spent."

"Okay. Well, how about we go get some ice cream?" Becky asked.

"Oh … yeah, sure let me ask my dad." Nicky shouted, "Dad we're going to Kilwoms, okay?"

"Okay Nicholas, but don't be too long," Nicky's dad yelled back.

Sue, Becky, and Nicky rode their bikes to the ice cream shop. It was a local hangout only ten minutes away on bike. Nicky was making sure that he didn't get too far ahead this time.

Kilwoms was always packed with kids on Saturdays, including Max and his posse of idiots. Max was still upset at what had happened in school last week.

As they walked in, Nicky saw them and knew things were not going to end well.

"So, how are you three girls doing?" Max asked.

"Watch your mouth, Tubby," Sue said angrily.

"Ooh, I'm scared. I guess you're the toughest of the three. I know little Nicky's a wimp." Max stared Nicky down.

Nicky briefly thought back to that beautiful tomahawk and what it could do. *"No, he's not worth the trouble,"* Nicky thought to himself.

"Are you ignoring me Sticky Nicky?" Max sometimes called him this because of an incident where Max glued Nicky's shoes to the ground in the fifth grade. "How about I glue your underwear to your ass cheeks this time?" All of Max's friends laughed.

"Come on, let's go," Becky said.

"Aww, did I hurt Sticky's feelings?" Max taunted.

Nicky knew he could hurt them all very badly if he chose to, but he decided to leave anyway. Unfortunately, Max didn't want to leave well enough alone. As Nicky, Sue, and Becky stepped outside and got on their bikes, Max and his friends followed.

"Hey Sticky, I don't know how you pulled off that trick back in school, but I'm not afraid of you." He kicked Nicky's bike making Nicky fall to the ground. Sue and Becky were being held by Max's friends.

"No! Stop it!" yelled Sue.

Max started kicking Nicky in the stomach. Nicky felt nothing, but he had to pretend he was being hurt. He remembered his father's words, *"Don't let them know."* Max kicked him again and again. Nicky pretended to be in pain, even yelling out.

"Stop!" yelled Becky, "You're hurting him."

"Come on Sticky. Scream again. Come on, cry!" But Nicky just laid on the ground. "Let's go," Max told his friends. "See ya later girls."

All the kids were staring at Nicky through the glass from the ice cream shop. Sue ran to Nicky who was still on the ground. "Are you okay?"

"Yeah, I'm fine. I just want to go home."

When Nicky arrived home he ran to his bedroom and cried. Not from physical pain as Max had no ability to physically hurt Nicky now, but from anger, humiliation and frustration.

"Someday I'll get that fat idiot alone. No, I can't hurt him. But, I can humiliate him." He thought of all the ways he could make Max feel the way he did.

"Nicholas!" Nicky heard his mom yell.

"Yeah, Mom?"

"Your lunch has been served. Please come to eat." Nicky's mom noticed his torn shirt from the earlier incident, but said nothing. "Was the food satisfactory Nicholas?"

"It was fine, Mom," Nicky answered. *"Man she's acting weird,"* Nicky thought to himself.

The next few days went okay for Nicky at school. He tried to avoid Max and his friends. He, Sue, and Becky had fun hanging out after school and playing basketball. But always in the back of Nicky's mind was Mr. Macken. When would the knock come and he'd have to go back to that "facility"?

One day after school, two loud knocks answered his question.

Chapter 18 - Return

"Mr. Macken! Welcome!" Nicky's dad said as he answered the door.

"Thank you Mr. Hernandez. Is Nicholas home?" Mr. Macken asked.

"Why yes he is. Nicholas? Mr. Macken is here," his dad called out to Nicky.

Nicky's stomach sank. He thought to himself, *"Oh no, I don't want to go back. I don't want to stay in that facility again."* He came out of his room to see Mr. Macken.

"Nicholas, it is good to see you again. Your parents have allowed another visit to our facility. Is that not great news?"

"Do I have to stay there overnight? Can't I come back home today?" Nicky asked.

"Well Nicholas, it is very far away, but I assure you, you will be back soon. Now get some clothes for a few days. I will be waiting outside."

"Nicholas, Mr. Macken only wants to help you. Do not worry. They can be trusted. Now, go get your things," Dad said.

Chapter 19 - Shock

Nicholas was escorted into another dark Prius by two men.
"Okay Nicholas, just like before we must darken the windows and
put up the divider."

"Where's Mr. Macken?"

"He is in another vehicle." A dark divider rose separating the
back seat from the front seats. Nicky could not see out of the side
windows either. A gas was released into the car, and after a few
minutes, Nicky was knocked unconscious.

Nicky awoke, once again, and found himself in his replicated
room from home. But this time, laid out on the dresser was a pair of
dark blue coveralls. *"Great. Now I get to look like all these other
guys. I wonder what tests they have for me now,"* Nicky thought to
himself.

Another unknown man with similar physical features to
everyone he'd encountered at the facility, entered the room.
"Nicholas, are you ready for the tests?"

"Yeah, I'm ready … let's go."

Nicky was led to a different room in the facility. Like most of the other rooms, this one had the same white lacquer like finish to every surface. However, it was much smaller measuring about ten feet long by ten feet wide. Mr. Macken was waiting for him.

"Hello Nicholas, these set of tests will be a little different than what we have done in the past," Mr. Macken explained.

"Okay, how are they different?"

"Well, most of today's tests will be less physical and more cerebral. Please sit. Now, close your eyes and extend your hand. Good." Mr. Macken pulled out a knife and slammed it down on Nicky's pinky, cutting it off.

"Ahhhh …!" Nicky screamed in dismay. "What did you do?!" But as Nicky cried, Mr. Macken asked him to look down. His finger had already begun to regenerate.

"I am sorry Nicholas, but I had to see if the curative process was viable. And apparently it was."

"But I don't understand," Nicky said puzzled.

"You see, Nicholas, we have experimented with a procedure so that you may heal in such a manner."

Nicky was still in shock, "But why hurt me?"

"Again, I apologize for my methods. I was almost sure the curative process would be successful."

"Almost sure! I don't want to be here anymore!" Nicky stood and shouted.

"Nicholas, please settle down. I will not hurt you again, I promise. Also, please understand your parents have signed waivers, so you must remain here until we are ready to send you home."

"My parents would never do that!" Nicky yelled angrily.

Mr. Macken was fully aware of what an angry Nicky was capable of doing. "They understand that your mission for your country is much larger than just you. Again I am terribly sorry. It will not happen again. You have my word. Now, please sit down." Nicky glared at Mr. Macken and reluctantly sat.

"Are you ready to continue?"

"Yes."

"Good, do you see that gentleman sitting down over there?" he pointed at a man sitting about fifty feet away.

"Yeah, I see him."

"Okay, now concentrate on his face and tell me what happens."

77

Nicky could hear a voice in his head, «Ten, nine, eight, seven, six, five, four, three, two, one.»

"I heard a voice counting down from ten," Nicky told Mr. Macken.

"Very good."

"Tell me how?" Nicky asked.

"Well, you have the ability to communicate telepathically with humans, not just animals."

"Wow, really? Can I make his mind explode like in the comic books?"

"No Nicholas, I am afraid not. You can only communicate. Now, please close your eyes. Do not worry. I am only testing your mind. You have my word. Picture total darkness in your mind. No sound, no feeling, only focus on your breathing. Now relax and listen to this word … ko-kí." Mr. Macken paused for a few seconds. "What do you see?"

Nicky started to become visibly disturbed. "I see a terrible war. Indians are being shot and are dying around me … I don't like this."

"Concentrate, Nicholas. Tell me what you see," instructed Mr. Macken.

"I don't want to see it anymore." Nicky opened his eyes. "What was that?" Nicky was sweating and breathing heavily.

"These are memories that you can recall from the essence that has merged with you."

"But I don't understand," Nicky said.

"These memories formed part of the life of a Native American who lived many years ago. You can access these memories," Mr. Macken explained.

"What? You said I had been merged with animals? What do you mean a Native American?"

"It is true Nicholas. You have been merged with a man. His essence is part of you now."

"How could this be? I don't want this. I don't want these memories. You have to reverse this."

"I am sorry for your distress Nicholas, but once the merger process has been finalized, there is no way to reverse it. You must learn to live with your new abilities and connections."

"But I don't want to."

"I am sure you will work it out. Well, Nicholas that is all for today, you may return to your room." Mr. Macken abruptly stopped the conversation.

Now back in his room, Nicky was still shaken by the images in his mind, the cutting off of his finger, and the knowledge that he was somehow merged with another man.

Nicky knew he was being monitored; he just sensed it. This was strange considering there were no visible cameras in the room. He yelled out, "Can I get an Xbox and a TV in here?"

An unknown voice could be heard through a speaker, "As you wish."

Video Games always had a way of clearing Nicky's mind, no matter how badly he felt.

"Thanks!"

Chapter 20 - Fun

Nicky stayed up almost all night playing on the X-box. Only a couple of hours of sleep later, someone knocked on the door.

"Good morning, Nicholas."

"Good morning pasty dude number 147," Nicky thought as he smirked. "I know, it's time to go," Nicky said.

When Nicky arrived at the Creation Room, Mr. Macken informed him things would be a little different today. "Nicholas, today I would like you to take over the Creation Room."

"Really?"

"Yes. Whatever you can imagine, the Creation Room will try to simulate. It is all yours. I will be back in a few hours."

The first thing Nicky thought of was a movie theater hooked up to an Xbox. "This is awesome!" After a couple of hours of playing Halo, he grew bored. Next he thought, *"Whitewater rafting on a jet ski? Why not?"* Drenched from the experience, he thought, *"What's next. Hang gliding!"* He was soaring over a mountainous area. When he finally landed he started to feel a little sad. He started thinking of those he missed so much.

Nicky tried to re-create home. He missed his family. He even created simulations of his parents. He hugged them, went outside to play some basketball with Sue and Becky, and finally he imagined their last trip and the cave that he fell into.

There it was, right in front of him, the cave. It scared him a little, but he was so curious he had to go in. *"Could it re-create what was in there?"* Nicky wondered. He jumped in the opening and walked until he saw it. The bones and the weapons were there just like he had seen so briefly in the cave before. *"Everything looks smaller than I remember,"* he thought.

"Interesting is it not, Nicholas?" he heard Mr. Macken's voice behind him.

Nicky jumped. "Yeah it is."

"Tell me Nicholas, why are you so curious about this place?"

"Well, I just wanted to see what's down here."

"I see. Well, since you are so curious, I suppose I should let you in on a little secret. We created the cave for a higher purpose."

"What do you mean you created it? For what? Some kind of trap?!"

"I would not necessarily categorize it as a trap. You see, many came before you. They were unable to survive the essence merging process. Some of their bones were discarded here as you can see." Mr. Macken pointed to them.

"But why?"

"To entice young curious types such as yourself."

"So the cave was created to trap kids so you could experiment on them? But … but … I could have died?"

"Well Nicholas, we do not use the word die. Your journey does not end when the vessel expires. It is simply a transition."

"You mean like the man and the animals that were merged with me?"

"Exactly. I promise, tomorrow all of your questions will be answered. Now, it has been a long day, please return to your room."

Nicky had many more questions, but decided it would be best to just listen to Mr. Macken, for now anyway.

Nicky spent the rest of the evening doing what he does most nights; reading comic books and playing X-Box until he passed out.

The next morning Nicky awoke to the sound of gas filling the room. Nicky's body was adapting to the gas. Larger and larger quantities of gas were needed each time it was used. But eventually his body relented. "Oh no. Not agai ..." Nicky was out. When he awoke he could not believe his eyes.

Part II

Today

Chapter 21 - Awakening

"Welcome back Nicholas!" As Nicky slowly opens his eyes, he looks around and sees the type of room he'd grown so accustomed to. It is cold and white, except now, there are three unusual structures above him that are clinging like stalactites to the ceiling. These structures are hanging three feet down and have an asperous rock like texture. Their metal like skin appears dull and faded. They look almost alive and seem to be slightly pulsating. At the tip of each is an ice blue, jagged crystal protruding from them like spears.

"This is our Essence Experimentation Room." Nicky hears Mr. Macken's voice. When he turns his head, he is shocked. Mr. Macken does not look human any longer! He, like several others in the room, are seven to eight feet tall, humanlike, but with elongated limbs. He looks like the stretched toy man Nicky remembers winning at a birthday party when he was younger. Their skin is similar to Nicky's own skin pigmentation, but has a kind of glowing, reddish-pink color. Their faces remind him of the famous painting he once saw online called 'The Scream.' But still, their humanlike faces are different in subtle ways. Nicky always thought aliens would look like the little, green men from the movies, not so much like us.

He looks down to see blue glowing restraints and notices two others about his age restrained as well. "What is this … what are you … and where am I?" Nicky was visibly shocked.

"Do not be distraught Nicholas; here is where we perfect the merging process. Unfortunately, many had to perish, but alas we have our three. That is William and that is Isabella over there. You three were the only ones who survived the merging process. So, we are studying why and what makes you three different. And yes, you may have guessed, we are not human. We have the ability to alter our physical appearance. I will answer all of your questions, but right now, experimentation must continue." A mask is placed over Nicky's face and after several minutes, Nicky sleeps.

Nicky wakes up again to hear a strange language, not verbalized, but just like with the animals he had encountered before; it is telepathic. Strangely, he can understand them. There are fifteen of them in the room now. Mr. Macken is speaking telepathically to William. It seems that William also has the ability to understand them. Mr. Macken senses when Nicky is awake, as if they are connected somehow.

"Ah, welcome back Nicholas, I know you are a curious one. So perhaps I may enlighten you on our origins as they pertain to your planet. Your own country was originally settled by Europeans, eventually pilgrims and puritans arrived at your shores to settle here. For the most part, they were in search of religious freedom.

"We had no such concept as religion, but we had a strong difference of opinion on our world regarding the topic of essence. Essence is what you humans refer to as spirit. You see Nicholas, when your vessel, or body has perished, your essence leaves its vessel. Where it may go we have not determined. Our essence remains in its vessel until it is transferred to another."

"You mean your spirit is stuck in your body until you get a new one?" Nicky asks.

"Precisely. On our planet we had the ability to create a new vessel."

"So, how do you die?" asks Nicky.

"We do not perish as humans do. Unfortunately, we are unable to create new vessels on your planet. We began
88

experimentation to transfer our essence to different vessels, be it human or animal, hundreds of years ago. We have not been successful yet, and are only limited to what you would consider 700 to 800 years in our current vessels. So we must be expeditious in our task."

"Seven hundred or 800 years! You guys live that long?"

Mr. Macken continues, "Yes it is true. I assume relative to humans, it is long. But there are other species Nicholas, where 700 or 800 years is a relative drop in the bucket, to use a human idiom."

"So if your body dies you're stuck in it until you can transfer your spirit?"

"Correct."

"Well, why not go back to your planet where a transfer is possible?"

"Unfortunately our transporter was destroyed when we landed here in the seventeenth century and our available aircraft are unable to travel into deep space. But even if we had the ability to travel there, we would not be welcome by those we left behind, and we would certainly be imprisoned. Leaving for a long period of time was unlawful. We do not procreate as easily as, for example, humans do.

"Again as stated," Mr. Macken continues, "We landed in your country at a tumultuous time. We were taken by the tenacity of the native people. Much like those Europeans who first landed here, we wish to acquire power and land so that we may eventually live in peace, without fear of humans and in our true forms. The forms you now see before you. As we learned from the Native Americans, we would never be accepted as we truly are. So by using our unique abilities, we have infiltrated all facets of the largest domestic and foreign governments and the most powerful companies on your planet. We simply take the essence of those in powerful positions, terminate their vessel and replace them, as your parents were."

Chapter 22 - Revelations

"What!? When!?"

"Well Nicholas, as you can imagine human parents seem to be unreasonably attached to the young vessels they produce. So we could not risk losing access to you. They were replaced before you arrived home after your first set of tests. Do not worry, they were not terminated."

"Where are they?"

"They are safe, Nicholas, but they are also being used for experimentation. Obviously, they created you, so we need to study their physiology, as we have your own."

"Please, let them go. It's us you want, not them."

"On the contrary, just as you three have been useful, your parents are also exceptionally useful to us. Again, as they created you, physiologically they must be studied."

Mr. Macken continued. "Our primary intent was always to transfer our essence to a human, so that we may endure. But over time our goals expanded. Very soon we will create an army of hundreds of thousands or perhaps millions of clones.

"You see, eventually we can shed the disgusting human disguises we are forced to use, and be free to be who we truly are. But in order to do that, we will need a powerful army. We are far too precious and few to be captured or disabled. And the best part is, we do not have to risk a single one of our brethren to accomplish our goals."

"So you think you're invincible? You will be exposed! I bet a bomb that was large enough could destroy you all!" Nicky interrupts angrily.

"Funny child, our essence can remain in fragments smaller than your most powerful forms of magnification could see," Mr. Macken's face suddenly changes. He becomes more intense. "I sense you mean to break free from your restraints. It is true that you are more powerful than any restraint we could construct. But these restraints are not there to simply restrain you. If you do break free, your parents would be instantaneously terminated. The restraints are connected directly to a material we call chryuk* (*Pronounced cry-yook) situated directly above their heads. It is similar in appearance

92

to an earthly crystal. We have tuned them specifically to your parent's brain waves. Amazing what the chryuk can do to human brain matter. If you did break free it would be a ghastly display indeed. I suggest you quell your impulsive nature and remain laying still, or there will not be much of your parent's remains to mourn."

Nicky's tense body relaxes. He can't risk breaking a restraint.

"You see Nicholas, we are far superior to you and your barbarous, primitive kind. But what we have been able to create with you three is beyond human. It is even beyond the Chreé*"

(*Pronounced kray-ee, what the aliens call themselves).

Mr. Macken continues, "When we are finally able to replicate the correct physiological conditions that have made you three possible, our army can grow. Individually, we may not be as powerful as you three, but we will reproduce large numbers making this obstacle immaterial.

"We have obviously learned to capture the essence of humans and animals. Mysteriously, your physical attributes became infinitely superior to the animal and human vessels who housed them."

"Why do I have these memories I don't want?" Nicky asks.

"That is another puzzle. Unfortunately, we have been unable to completely remove the most recent life experiences of the spirits, as you call them, but hope to soon. Ahh ... well I see we are ready for the final procedures."

"But ..."

Mr. Macken turns his head. "Full concentration, this may be our last opportunity to anesthetize him. His body is recovering too quickly now," he instructs an assistant. The mask is placed over Nicky's face and after a few minutes, Nicky goes to sleep. "Good night, Nicholas."

Nicky awakens in his replicated room. His head is pounding.

«Welcome back, Nicholas.» He hears Mr. Macken in his head.

«You gave us quite a scare in our final enhancement procedures. You are much too important to lose now.» Mr. Macken continues, «As you can imagine, telepathy and many other enhancements are not human or earthly animal traits. We have been experimenting with our own essence. We have merged the essence of Chreé with you three. To our astonishment it has exceeded our expectations.»

«Wouldn't you lose one of your own when you merge?» Nicky asks.

«Only a piece of our essence is necessary. This would not be possible with your kind. Now Nicholas, I am needed elsewhere. But before I go, I must warn you again, if you make any attempt at an escape, your parent's lives will be terminated. Do you understand?»

«I understand ... but how do I know they're okay?» Nicky asks.

«You don't. Will you chance it?»

«No ... I will not.»

Finally Nicky is left alone to think. *"Why is this happening to me? I just want to be home. I want everything to go back to normal."*

What seems like weeks have passed since Nicky was threatened. The physically demanding training and assessing of his strength, speed, agility, and even tolerance to pain and extreme weather conditions are endless. Nicky is a prisoner, but he reluctantly obliges because the cost is too great if he does not. *"I can't take any more Xbox and this stupid room, but I can't risk my parent's lives. How can I free them? I have to figure out where they are,"* he thinks.

«Nicholas?» Mr. Macken's voice comes through in Nicky's mind. «Would you like to meet William and Isabella?»

Chapter 23 - Together

Nicky is summoned to the Creation Room. He finally gets to meet Isabella and William.

When he walks in, they instantly hug. It is as if they knew each other all of their lives. Nicky finally gets a close up view of their faces, he notices similar features. Nicky thought Isa and Willy might even be twins.

"Call me Nicky."

"I'm William and this is Isabella, but you can call us Willy and Isa. And no, we are not related."

"Really? But ... Wow, okay ... anyway I'm so happy to finally see you upright and not laying on some stupid bed strapped down," Nicky declares.

"We are too," Willy responds.

"So, do they have your pare ..." Nicky starts saying before Willy interrupts.

"Shhh ..." Nicky feels something strange in his mind like someone is trying to telepathically communicate with him.

"Go ahead and let me 'link' with your mind," Willy whispers.

"Okay … I guess, how?"

"Just allow it to be, don't fight it."

Nicky suddenly hears Willy's voice in his head. «We have learned to communicate where only we can hear each other. It's almost like an encrypted signal, you allow me to 'link' with your mind and we can communicate without others listening in.»

«You're sure?» Nicky asks.

«Yeah, don't worry it's kind of like whispering,» Willy explains.

All three hear Mr. Macken's voice interrupt telepathically. «Nicholas, William, and Isabella, please prepare for more assessments.»

The room changes to a replication of Washington, DC. They are suddenly on a six lane street only miles from the White House. Eerily, there are no cars or people. They are just surrounded by stone store fronts. "We will simulate some attacks. Defend yourselves," A voice can be heard over a speaker.

A bow and arrow, a war club, and a tomahawk appear.

They all have a different favorite: Nicky the tomahawk, Willy the war club, and Isa the bow and arrow. Four soldiers appear carrying only knives.

"Guess we'll all take one. Whoever's fastest gets the last one," Willy tells Nicky and Isa smiling.

Isabella took off faster than the other two. "They merged her with a horse, so she's a little faster than we are. But I've got these." Willy smiles showing Nicky what looks like blue, glowing fangs. "Let's go. I'll show you how to do that later."

It was over in seconds. The soldiers disappear after they were neutralized.

"Wow! You guys are good," Nicky shouts.

"Yeah, we've been here longer, but you'll get as fast as we are at stopping them," Isa explains.

"You know why they're testing us?" Nicky asks.

"Yeah, but let's not talk about it now," answers Willy.

"Oh no, here comes a tank!" Nicky yells.

Chapter 24 - Boom

"We've never simulated this," Willy remarks and suddenly, BOOM! The explosion shakes the ground. A projectile comes flying through the air from the tank's main gun. All three can see the projectile as it speeds towards them. They all jump out of the impact area. The explosion destroys several store fronts and creates a large crater in the road.

Nicky, out of anger, instinctively roars taking out buildings directly behind the tank and destroying the tank's engine. Smoke can be seen rising from the rear of the tank.

"Whoa, you'll have to teach us that one," Isa says amazed at Nicky's unique weapon.

"I thought we all had the same gifts?" Nicky replies. But before Isa could speak again, another round fires from the main gun towards Isa and Nicky, again forcing them to jump out of the way.

«I'm on the tank!» Willy yells. «I see the hatch!» Willy begins to tear at the hinge extending what looks like blue glowing claws, sinking them into the tank's hatch. With one howl, he rips it open. The tank driver disappears with one quick strike.

"Phew, man that was scary," Nicky says.

"Yeah those explosions felt real to me," Isa exclaims startled.

"Do you think we can get hurt? I thought these were all simulations," Nicky asks.

"I don't know. I think they want us alive. But Mr. Macken is crazy," Isa smiles.

Willy suddenly runs to them, "Man that was scary."

"Hey, I just said that," Nicky says.

Nicky and Isa laugh. "You've got to show me that claw trick," Nicky tells Willy.

"Only if you show me that roaring trick of yours," Willy replies.

"Hey, wait a minute, guys," Isa interrupts. "Do you hear that? Something really big is coming."

Chapter 25 - Topple

"Soldiers are coming, we need to link now," says Willy.

«Okay guys, adapt.»

«Wait! What do you mean?» Nicky asks.

«Oh no! He hasn't learned that ability yet,» Isa tells Willy.

«The rumble is getting closer!» Willy yells.

«Okay, Nicky, look behind you. What do you see?» Isa asks.

«A wall. Why?» Nicky replies.

«Now imagine your skin looking like that wall. Do it now!» Isa yells.

«Okay, I'm trying, but … wait … I'm … I'm changing but how?» Nicky exclaims.

«No time … now, put your back to the wall,» Isa instructs Nicky.

«I'm almost … invisible,» Nicky says.

«Well it's not perfect, but hopefully they won't notice,» Isa tells Willy.

«They're here! There's thousands of them,» Willy says peeking around a wall. «It's a military brigade!»

Nicky and Isa also take a look around the wall, staring down New York Avenue, a wide four lane road. Thousands of infantry soldiers and four tanks advance towards them. Two tanks are in front and two are behind the brigade.

«How do we stop this?» Nicky asks.

«I don't know,» Willy replies.

«Wait. Nicky, your roar, can you take down a large building?»

«I don't know ... maybe, why?» Nicky asks.

«If you could collapse large buildings on them, we have a shot, and downtown is our only option. If my plan doesn't work, we'll have to face an entire brigade. We have to get downtown, let's go ... remember Nicky, concentrate on your surroundings to adapt to them,» Willy says.

«Okay, I'll try,» Nicky replies.

They move carefully along the walls so they are not spotted. Nicky is not as proficient yet at adapting his body. And at times he is not adapting to his surroundings correctly. Intermittently he changes back to his real body; he resembles a flickering TV.

Ever the curious one, Nicky just has to ask a question as they move covertly towards the downtown area.

«How am I changing the way my clothes look? I understand our skin, but how's this possible?» Nicky asks.

«We can affect not just are own bodies, but any matter we touch. Right now we can only change small objects, but who knows, maybe in time we can change larger objects,» Isa tells Nicky as they move down the streets.

«Amazing!»

«Okay guys, we'll talk more about it later. You have to focus on adapting Nicky,» Willy interrupts.

After a few minutes, they are finally in position downtown. They are just outside one of the tallest buildings in the downtown area, about a mile ahead of the brigade.

"I don't know if I can do this," Nicky says, suddenly feeling apprehensive.

«We believe in you. You're our brother now. And we'll help you anyway we can,» Isa reassures Nicky.

«I remember watching a demolition special on the Discovery Channel. If we could damage some of the support beams facing the street, it will be much easier for you to topple the buildings on them. I say we take these three buildings.» Willy points towards the three tallest buildings next to each other.

Nicky and Isa agree.

«We'll have to time it perfectly. Luckily, we don't need radios,» Isa smiles.

«Awesome. Let's do this,» Nicky says.

All three get into position.

The troops slowly push north; they're marching in between the four tanks. Willy and Isa wait inside the first southernmost of the three tall buildings they plan on toppling. Nicky is just outside the same building peeking around the corner, waiting to give the signal.

«They're almost in position. Okay … ready on three. One, two, three go!» Nicky yells.

Willy and Isa start running through the inside of the empty building, destroying the support columns as they run through them. Finally, they simultaneously crash through the outer wall.

«Now!» Isa yells.

A growl more powerful than Nicky has never done before, erupts from his gut. It's so loud that it shakes the ground, and so powerful that the first large building topples over in seconds; hundreds of replicated troops disappear. Quickly, they do the same to the last two large buildings until none of the soldiers are left.

"We did it!" Nicky yells. They are overjoyed.

"I can't believe it! We did it! That was amazing!" Willy screams!

The three new friends hug. The Creation Room goes back to white and telepathically they hear Mr. Macken, «I believe you three are finally ready.» Nicky just stands, perplexed by this statement.

Chapter 26 - Birth

Sitting in their replicated rooms early the next day, Isa, Nicky, and Willy are communicating securely linked.

«So, maybe if I touch my bed I can change it? Let's see.» Nicky closes his eyes and concentrates. «Why isn't it changing?» Nicky wonders.

«Well, we can't change large objects yet. Try something smaller. Do you have a lamp?» Isa asks Nicky.

«Yeah,» Nicky responds.

«Touch it and imagine it as something about the same size,» Isa suggests.

«Okay.» Nicky closes his eyes, touches the lamp, and thinks of a toaster. Amazingly the lamp transforms into a toaster. "Whoa!"

«Now, let it go,» Isa instructs.

«It changed back to normal.» Nicky just has to do it over and over again. «This is so cool!»

«Yeah, I guess we're used to it,» Isa laughs.

«So, what do you think Mr. Macken meant by 'we're ready'?» Nicky asks.

«They intend on trying to clone us now. They wanted to know what we were capable of. Up to now they've been unsuccessful in finding bodies, or vessels, as they call them, they could use. Unfortunately they're much closer to having an army now,» Willy says.

«How do you know all of this?» Nicky asks.

«Z told us. He's one of them but doesn't believe what his kind is doing is right. So he's trying to help us. He told us that they intend on first controlling the American government and then eventually all of humanity. They've learned many things from our wars, especially from the Nazis.»

«But what about our allies?» asks Nicky.

Willy goes on to explain, «They've already infiltrated every large government in the world. We'll have no allies. The objective is not to take control by force, but to eventually take control internally. In other words, control our government from the inside. With this strategy, they believe we will be much more easily deceived. They plan to promise the masses changes to government programs that would enhance their lives at no cost to them, not knowing the true cost.»

«I can't believe how deep this goes.» Nicky is stunned by all this information.

«Z also taught us how to adapt, link, and a few other things. He even told us why they left their planet,» Isa tells Nicky.

«Mr. Macken told me it was about a disagreement on essence,» Nicky states.

«I guess you could say that. The Chreé can sense when their bodies are close to dying. They created bodies by using a large living organism called the Chrymisium.* (*Pronounced, Cry-mis-ee-um.) They did this during what they call a creation ceremony.

«The Chrymisium looks like a giant, brilliant, blue crystal that hung from the ceiling like a stalactite. Ten or so Chreé would enter the chamber where the Chrymisium was. They would start chanting and then a piece of each of their essence would enter the Chrymisium. It would get really bright and a blue gelatinous liquid would start to drip from the Chrymisium until a body was created. They could then use this body to transfer their essence to whenever one of their own bodies died.»

Nicky shudders, «Huh … confusing and creepy.»

«I know; it gets better. So, here's why they left. They also used to have what they called a birthing ceremony. After the creation ceremony they would start to chant again, and all but one of the Chreé would turn around. The one who remained facing the basin was called the birther. He would send as much of his essence as was necessary to the Chrymisium until a much larger amount of the blue gelatinous liquid fell from it. Once the Chrymisium stopped glowing, a new life was created. They had to be careful, if too much of the Chreé's essence was needed, his entire essence was lost in the Chrymisium for eternity,» Isa says.

«But after some time, the birthing ceremony was outlawed. Those in power thought enough Chreé had been created and no more would be necessary. The birthing ceremony was never performed again. That is what started the exodus from their planet. Those who wanted the birthing ceremony to continue, set out for a planet they could start over in,» Willy adds.

«I think I get it. So, without the Chrymisium, they can't create a body or create others like them?» Nicky asks.

«Right. That's why they are so desperate to make a human transfer possible. But first they want control. They want to clone us to help finalize their plans. They want to use us to help them destroy our own government, and eventually all governments.» Willy explains.

Chapter 27 - Introduction

«Nicky! Wake up!» It was early the next day when Nicky hears Willy's voice linked. «I'd like you to speak to Z.»

«Okay.»

«Think of this as the coolest conference call ever,» Willy smiles.

«Hello Nicholas,» Z's voice comes in deep. Nicky could immediately feel his essence; it feels like positive energy. A very different feeling than Nicky got from all the other Chreé he'd encountered.

«I have so many questions.»

Z laughs. «I know Nicky. I have been following you for a while now.»

«Wait ... you were the light, weren't you?»

«Yes. I tried to get to you before the others.»

«That must have been you outside my window. I'm sorry,» Nicky apologizes.

«Yes that was also me! You have quite a powerful auditory weapon. I was so pleased you pulled through the initial merger.»

«Can you tell me about my parents? How are they doing?»

«They are fine. They have been placed in what you would consider a sleep-like state. They have been in suspended animation since their arrival, just like Isa and Willy's parents,» Z explains.

«Thank God! How can we rescue them?» Nicky asks.

«This will be very difficult and you must prepare. Perhaps Mr. Macken, as you call him, could be persuaded to continue your training. That would be most helpful for the operation we must undertake. As you know, we have the ability to transform our bodies to replicate human form, but you three have somehow developed the capability to not only transform your own bodies but external matter. It is extraordinary; continue to practice this gift. Also, you can ma ... wait ... I must go.»

«But ... what happened!?» Nicky exclaims.

«It's okay,» Isa says. «He has to be careful. If he's even suspected of helping us we're all dead.»

«I think Z is right. We need more training, but even then I don't know if it will work,» mentions Willy.

Nicky turns to Willy, «Can you tell me how you create those weapons, those fangs and claws?»

«Well, since I was merged with a grey wolf, I try to access him,» Willy explains.

«What do you mean?» Nicky asks.

«Well, Z told us we could access these parts because subconsciously, we can use trigger words. So if I think the word ba-chú, the Apache word for wolf, I connect with him and somehow create what you saw. For you the word is...»

«Wait I know,» Nicky interrupts. «It is Sũsh, for bear. But how do I know that?»

«The essence of the great warriors we were fused with makes it possible for us to speak their language,» Isa answers.

«Now say the word and concentrate on the connection. Close your eyes and say it,» Willy says.

«Okay.» Nicky breathes deeply, "Sũsh," and a flood of memories rush to him; roaming, feeding, being captured, and even the merge.

«Now become him, imagine the teeth, imagine the claws,» Willy says.

Slowly, enormous grizzly claws and teeth materialize with a blue glow. But Nicky just feels anger. He can't concentrate on anything but hurting those *things*, those aliens!

«Close your eyes, Nicky, come back to yourself. Relax, breathe,» Willy instructs him.

After a few minutes, Nicky composes himself. «I couldn't control my anger.»

«It takes time. You will learn to accept it, but you can't really control it. And that's okay, it gets better on its own, the more you bring him up,» explains Willy. «It just takes time and of course we can manifest other things.»

«Like what?» Nicky asks.

«Well …»

Chapter 28 - Connection

Isa asks Nicky, «What does 'Chǐdn-tú-yo' mean?»

«I know, that means Spirit land,» Nicky replies.

Isa goes on to explain, «This word can connect you to the essence of the man you merged with. From what we know, the Chreé were fond of the Apache and took only the greatest warrior's spirits. That's who we've merged with. If we focus and connect, we can also manifest weapons. For me the bow and arrow, the club for Willy, and …»

«The tomahawk for me,» Nicky interrupts. «It was my favorite, but how do I do this? I don't want the bad memories.»

«First focus on the tomahawk, pretend it's in your hand. Really feel it. See it. Now say it in your mind,» Isa says

"Chǐdn-tú-yo," Nicky thinks. Instant darkness encompasses Nicky.

«Don't fear. Only focus on the weapon in your hand. Do it. Open your eyes.»

«It's here! It's here! I see it! It's glowing blue! It's beautiful. Wait … I see a woman and children. They're hurt or dead!» A tear starts running down Nicky's face.

«Nicky relax. Let it go, let it go,» Isa says.

«Okay, okay. It's gone. The memories too.»

«Just like the bear you have to keep going back. It will happen in time. You will be able to control the memories, but you have to learn not to fight them, simply accept them. Eventually they won't bother you anymore. Practice these powers; you will need them against these monsters.»

«Nicholas, I see you have been practicing in your room.» Mr. Macken's voice interrupts telepathically.

"Damn. He's been watching me," Nicky thinks.

«How did you learn to manifest a tomahawk?» Mr. Macken asks.

«Well, I just dreamt about it and when I woke up I did it!»

"I hope he buys this story," Nicky thinks to himself.

«Interesting. Well, keep practicing.»

«I will.»

"I'll keep practicing to make sure I get rid of you," Nicky

thinks.

Chapter 29 - Escape

Several hours later, Z returns and links to the three, «Well, I apologize for my hasty exit. Discretion is paramount. What did he say to you Nicky?» asks Z.

«He's watching me. He asked how I learned to manifest a tomahawk,» Nicky answers.

«I see. So, you are able to manifest a tomahawk now. Excellent. You are learning. Your potential is extraordinary. Unfortunately, I have terrible news. They intend to place you three in suspended animation much quicker than we had anticipated,» Z tells them.

«When?» Isa asks.

«Tomorrow. Escape must happen tonight.»

«Tonight!? But how, Z? How can we escape when we've been kept in the dark about the layout of this place?» Willy asks.

«Calm yourself. Remember you will have my guidance,» Z replies. «At exactly 2:22 a.m. your doors will open. I will guide you out, where hopefully, you can escape.»

«And what about our parents?» Isa asks.

«Their escape will have to wait. I am sorry. I cannot make this operation work and help with your parent's extraction simultaneously. Our only course of action at this point is for you three to attempt an escape. I see no reason for your parents to be harmed. Do not concern yourself with their safety. I will make sure they are safe. If you want to help them, you will follow this course or all will all be lost, including perhaps, your planet as you know it.»

«We know you'll keep them safe Z,» Willy says.

«Thank you. Now get some rest. It will be necessary to be at your best,» Z tells them.

Chapter 30 - Time

«I can't sleep and it's 1:59 a.m.,» Nicky says.

«I know, same here,» Willy replies.

«What about you, Isa? I sense you're sad and scared,» Nicky says.

«Yeah, I am. But I know we can do this,» Isa smiles. «I sense your fear, too. So I guess we're connected now.»

«Yeah, we're all scared, but you're right we can do this,» Nicky agrees.

«Just in case we don't, I'm proud to call you guys my family now,» Willy says.

2:01 a.m.

«Nicky?» Willy calls out.

«Yeah?» Nicky responds.

«Remember, focus on your weapons. Try ... at least for now, not to get caught up in the memories. Okay? Just focus on what we have to do.»

Nicky nods, «Got ya.»

2:20 a.m.

«Guys, thanks for being with me and all of your help. I love you guys,» Nicky says.

«Let's save the love for when we're out of this dump,» Willy smiles.

«It's 2:21 a.m. It's almost time,» Isa announces.

Chapter 31 - Escape

Z comes through telepathically. «There are three Watchers. They are connected to each other much like your surveillance cameras, but the images are fed to their minds. I will distract their minds long enough so that you can step out and adapt your vessel to its surroundings.»

«Got it. We'll disappear as soon as we're out,» Isa responds.

2:22 a.m.

All three doors open simultaneously. «Quickly, all step out and adapt to the white hall,» Z instructs them.

Nicky had been practicing and had gotten much better at adapting. All three are together again in the hallway. All three rooms are next to each other and they never even knew it. They can't help but laugh quietly.

«They would never suspect an escape. So there are no extra security measures. Now go left and down the hall quickly!» Seconds later, « Are you at the T yet?» Z asks.

«Yes, we're here,» Willy answers.

«Right. Go.» Z continues to direct them.

«Stop!» Nicky yells. All quickly put their backs against the wall. One of the Chreé passes right in front of them.

Isa immediately blocks any attempts to sense them.

«Clear,» Nicky says.

«Continue straight to the door at the end of the hall,» a double door opens, «Now go!» They enter a large hall. «Go to the fourth door on your right.» All three hurry.

They have entered another hallway with several white doors.

«Do these guys ever paint anything but white?» Nicky asks.

«Quickly to the third door on your left,» Z instructs.

The three enter.

«But it's just an empty room,» Isa says.

Suddenly, a small panel opens in one of the walls. «Go!» Z instructs.

Willy pauses, «Oh man, I'm kind of claustrophobic.»

«No time. Let's go!» Isa yells.

All three get on their hands and knees.

«You can return your vessel to normal. There are no Watchers here,» says Z. They stop adapting to their surroundings.

They continue down into the cramped, pitch-black chute for miles.

«Have you reached the end?» Z questions after several minutes.

Luckily their enhanced eyes can see in complete darkness.

«Yes, we've reached the end,» Willy replies.

«Excellent. Now you will have to dig out. Break the chute and dig. You are about twelve feet below the surface. Perhaps Willy's wolf merger would suit him for this task,» Z suggests.

«Okay. I'll dig us out.» Willy's glowing claws appear and light up the dark chute. At speeds not visible to the human eye, Willy starts to dig. After a few seconds they ascend to the desert floor.

All three now stand in the dark, desolate desert looking up at the star-lit sky.

«Nothing but desert ... where are we?» Isa asks.

«You are in the New Mexico desert now. I must go and will be unable to communicate with you for some time. I do not know how much time all of you have before your escape is noticed. Good luck and stay strong.» Z breaks his link.

"We're out! We're out!" They start jumping and laughing.

Then they realize something.

"You know we're in the middle of nowhere. Now what?"

Nicky asks.

Chapter 32 - X

"First, let's mark the spot. I get the feeling we'll need to use this chute again real soon. Let's drop some large cactus here in the form of an X," Willy says.

They search and find a cactus large enough to be noticed. They return and drop two large cacti over the chute exit.

"Well, we can't stay here all night. Do you guys see that road? Looks like maybe, five miles? Let's go. And guess who'll get there first." Isa winks at Willy and Nicky.

The race is on. After a few seconds, Isa arrives first. Nicky and Willy are almost tied behind her.

"Wow! You're fast!" Nicky tells Isa.

"We're all really fast. Unfortunately, she is just a little bit faster. Of course the wolf has the most stamina, so I can go the farthest without passing out," Willy smiles.

"So, if the Chreé are in human form, how do we know who's Chreé and who's human?" Nicky asks.

"I can sense them," Isa answers.

"Yeah she's also more sensitive telepathically than we are. Ever heard of a horse's sixth sense?" Willy asks.

"Amazing how it's manifested differently in all of us," Nicky mentions. "I wonder what my unique gifts are."

Isa looks at Nicky, "Well, just like every animal is unique, so are many of our gifts. You'll find yours … like the roar."

Willy's face suddenly turns visibly dejected. "All I can think about are my parents. We have to go back. We need a plan."

With his stomach growling, Nicky looks at Isa and Willy, "I say first we eat. I wonder if there's a place with fish sticks around here."

"Do you ever stop thinking about eating?" Isa asks Nicky.

"Yeah, usually when I'm playing on the Xbox."

Chapter 33 - Fast

The three escapees walk along the main strip of this small town for a few minutes before lights begin to approach.

"Let's get a ride," Willy says as he extends his thumb.

A gray haired, leathery faced man who has worked too many years out in the sun stops and agrees to give them a ride. They all jump into the back of his faded red 1970's Chevy pickup truck. They figured three kids running faster than a jet down the center of this small town might look suspicious, this was a better option. About ten minutes later they arrive

"Thanks again," Nicky tells the driver, as they all jump out of the truck bed.

They walk into a local twenty-four hour Denny's restaurant. They pick a booth towards the back facing the entrance. They are the only ones in the restaurant at this time of night.

"What can I get you kids?" the waitress asks.

"Could we just get water for now?"

"Sure."

"Hey we don't have any money," Isa whispers.

"Don't worry about that," Willy replies.

"You know once they know we're gone, they'll be expecting us to come back for our parents," Nicky says.

"Yeah, Z is our only hope of keeping them safe," Willy says.

"Are there others that think like Z?" Nicky asks Willy.

"I don't know. He never told us, but I don't think he could do it alone," Willy replies.

"Wait. Stop talking. I sense a Chreé near us," Isa says startled.

Suddenly, under the table Willy's claws and Nicky's tomahawk manifest. The table below them is now glowing blue.

"Get ready," Willy says.

"No. Stop! He's friendly. I don't sense he's like the others," Isa says.

"Is it Z?" Willy asks.

"I don't know, but here he comes." The Chreé who is in human form walks through the entrance and immediately approaches their booth. He drops a note on their table and walks away. Isa picks it up.

"What does it say?" Nicky asks.

130

Isa reads the note, "Interesting, it says they still don't know we're gone."

"Well, it's still the middle of the night. What else does it say?" Willy asks.

"Look up to the cross. Wait until 6:00 a.m."

"Let's go. Sorry we have an emergency!" Willy yells out to the waitress as they step outside.

The bald eagle is unique. It is the only animal to be merged with all of them. Native Americans considered the bald eagle to be a god of the sky. Like all their other senses, their vision was far beyond even that of the eagle's vision. Many miles away, they all see a large pink cross, and instantly they know that's where they need to be.

"We'll run through the desert so no one can spot us. Oh, and slow down, will ya?" Nicky tells Isa.

"Yeah, sure, I'll slow down a little for you," Isa winks and runs off.

"Man, she's fast," Nicky says.

"I know, I know," Willy responds. "Now let's go!"

After a few seconds, the three arrive at the church. It looks like it came out of an old western movie. They enter the old, unlocked church. The rickety wood floors creek under the weight of their feet. The peeling paint and musky odors are the only things to greet them.

"How about we get some rest," Willy suggests as he sits down in an empty, unkempt pew.

"Good idea …" Nicky and Isa choose a pew and try to get some sleep.

6:00 a.m.

The church's double doors open. Behind them a man dressed as a priest enters. He morphs back in to a Chreé. They all sense the same thing; it was Z. They all hug him.

"So good to see you all, but I have some bad news. You must return immediately. We felt your parents would be safe even after my brethren discovered you three had escaped. We miscalculated. They are now at great risk. Retrieving your parents will not be an easy task. I fear for your lives, but I cannot jeopardize others who are sympathetic to our cause. I will help you enter their chambers, but you will be on your own once you have retrieved your parents. Do you understand?"

"We understand. So if we're discovered, we'll have to fight our way out?" Nicky asks.

"Yes. We have no choice. You must save them now. I fear our window is closing. Return to the chute location. We will link when you arrive."

"Okay Z, thanks," Willy replies.

"Let's go!" Isa tells them.

Chapter 34 - Again

They don't care if they're spotted now. They run faster than they ever have and arrive in seconds.

Just outside the chute, the kids reestablish their link.

«Well, we got out easy enough. Why not go back in?» Nicky smiles.

«Come on. Let's go. This should be fun,» Willy says.

They remove the cacti covering the hole.

«Let's see what all that training was for,» Isa says. They jump down.

«Okay Z, we're in the chute,» Willy reports.

«Quickly, back to the room where you first entered the chute.» The three make their way back through the chute. «Now follow the same path back to your rooms,» Z instructs.

The three adapt their bodies to remain unseen.

«Okay, we're in the hallway.»

«Now continue straight to the T and make a left this time.»

They move quietly, but at a brisk pace. «Continue down the hall to the end; do you see the green glowing light above the door?» Z asks.

«Yes, we see it,» Willy replies.

«Now enter quietly. There will be perhaps ... six or seven Chreé in the room. You must not be detected or all is lost.»

Suddenly, the doors automatically open. They quickly enter and immediately place themselves against the wall. Three Chreé turn around and approach them. Isa begins to block any telepathic attempts by the Chreé to sense them. They walk up to the open door.

"Strange," one Chreé says to the other in their native language.**(**- Chreé Language)

"Indeed," another replies and simply walks back to the machines they were tending to.**

In typical Chreé fashion, this room is nothing but white, except this room had machines made out of a thin Plexiglas like material along the walls. In front of this material are colorful floating images and words in the Chreé language. The three innately understand the Chreé language floating approximately one eighth of an inch in front of the material. They carefully sneak past the Chreé working on the machines.

"Phew," Nicky thinks. They all could breathe again.

«Now, there should be steps straight ahead. Do you see them?» Z asks.

«Yes,» Willy replies.

«Go!» Z responds.

They descend into another long, white hallway.

«Careful. All areas are watched,» Z says. «All of your parents will be in the room through the fourteenth door to your right.»

When they arrive, the doors automatically open. There lay the parents, all sleeping. Their parents' wrists and ankles are strapped down with a leather like rich, brown material. Just like the kids, they are strapped to steel beds.

Their restraints suddenly disappear in to the bed. «Touch the blue Chryuk above their heads until they turn green,» Z says.

All three can't help but smile when they see their parent's faces. They all touch the blue glowing Chryuk above their heads. When they turn green their parents slowly begin to wake up. Nicky hears his name being uttered groggily, "Nicky?"

For the first time in a long time Nicky hears his father's voice,

"Nicky … is … is that you?"

Chapter 35 - Reunited

All of the parents are awake and tears of joy flow. The parents and the kids are overjoyed. Hugs exchange all around.

The moment they had all waited for has finally arrived. But, before they can celebrate too much, Z begins speaking to the kids, «I'm sorry to interrupt, but we must evacuate with haste.»

"Okay, we have to go," Nicky tells everybody.

"Where are we?" Isa's dad asks.

"Long … long story Dad, but we have to go now. Follow us," Isa says.

«I must stop communicating with you now. Remember your parents will be seen by the Watchers as soon as you step out of the doors,» Z warns them.

As they approach, the doors open. Willy takes one step outside, which triggers a noise like they have never heard before.

"Cover your ears!" Isa yells.

The Watchers' screams were so intense, they pierce their covered ears. The screams stop and four Chreé guards appear.

«What do we do now?» Nicky asks. «This is for real.»

«I don't know. We've only done simulations; we have never really fought anyone,» Isa interrupts.

Willy answers, «We have to do this. To immobilize the body, we must decapitate them. If not, they will regenerate. And if we're captured, they'll kill us all.»

Suddenly, the four Chreé hold hands and a pulse of blue light rushes towards the kids and their parents. The parents are knocked out. The kids fall to the ground, but immediately get back up.

«What was that?» Nicky asks. It felt like pure energy.

«I don't know, but we have to stop them, now!» Willy yells.

Nicky manifests a tomahawk and with one throw, two aliens are decapitated. Their bodies collapse and they begin to glow a light blue hue.

Isa's legs transform into legs like that of the Palomino horse glowing with Essence. She runs up the wall, jumps off, and with a single kick decapitates the final two.

«Nice … hey, you look like a horse,» Nicky tells Isa.

«Really!?» Isa says sarcastically, «Oh great, my new shoes are destroyed.»

«No time for fashion. Let's go,» Willy says.

Willy, Isa, and Nicky each pick up their parents and throw them over their shoulders. They begin to run down another white hallway, then up the stairs to the large room with the green light above the door. When they enter, nine more Chreé are waiting, glowing with anger.

«We have to put our parents down,» Isa says.

«If they touch them, their souls could be lost,» Willy points out.

«Just by one touch?» Nicky asks.

«Yes. We must protect them at all costs,» Willy replies.

Another large, blue pulse hits Isa. She isn't expecting it. It knocks her to the ground. Nicky's powerful growl knocks out three of the Chreé. Willy manifests a war club. The aliens begin to pulse blue energy. All three jump out of the way. Willy jumps towards two Chreé using his club. With a single hit, they fall. Isa jumps high, avoiding a pulse with amazing agility, lands and knocks three more out with swift kicks. One more tomahawk slash by Nicky and the last one is down.

«Those that are knocked out will probably heal soon. Let's hurry,» Willy says with urgency.

The kids pick up their parents again.

«We'll have to drag them through the chute; it's going to be a long trip,» Isa states.

«I know and we can't risk hurting them. We'll have to go slowly,» Willy replies.

After a long trip in pitch black, the three finally arrive at the end of the chute.

When they begin their ascent to the surface, Willy yells, «Oh no, trouble!»

Chapter 36 - Spotted

When Willy peeks just above the surface, he sees two flying aircraft. He had never seen anything like it before. They are oblong, black, and shiny like polished rocks. They are silent with no windows or doors that he could see.

Isa tells Willy, «I sense they're looking for us. We can't let them find the chute. That may implicate Z.»

«Let's go,» Willy yells.

They all pull their parents out of the chute. With their parents draped over their shoulders, they try to run away from the ships.

«Too late!» Isa yells.

One of the Chreé ships turns around and spots them.

«Spread apart,» Willy says.

The ship pulses, and it's followed by an explosion. Nicky jumps out of the way. A crater where the pulse exploded could be seen. Isa manifests a bow and arrow. She shoots an arrow that penetrates the ship damaging it. Isa senses the ship is unmanned.

«The Watchers must be flying the ships back at the facility where we were held,» Isa tells them.

Nicky jumps thirty feet in the air with a tomahawk in hand. He drives it through the ship. The ship comes crashing to the ground.

«Run!» Willy screams.

«Try the church. Maybe Z will be there, but remember don't go too fast. I don't know if our parent's bodies can handle the speed,» Willy says.

The three travel at a much slower pace than they're used to. After running for what seemed like an eternity, the group finally arrives at the church.

Chapter 37 - Awaken

"It's empty," says Isa.

"Let's just contact Z," says Nicky.

"We can't risk linking with Z, even secure communication could put him at risk," Isa explains.

"How?" Nicky asks.

"They can't hear us, but any Chreé close enough to Z might be able to sense a secure link has been made and I'm sure even that is forbidden right now," Willy explains.

"I guess we just wait then," says Nicky.

Isa, Willy, and Nicky's parents are still out cold from the pulse.

"Isa, can you help our parents?" Willy asks.

"I don't know, I'll try." Isa closes her eyes to concentrate and instinctively touches her parents' foreheads. Like the palomino horse whose essence is now within her, her intuitiveness is more developed than the others. They awaken and happily embrace again. Isa then awakens all of the parents.

Nicky's dad still wants some answers.

Still woozy, Nicky's dad asks, "What's going on?"

"Remember all the strange things that happened to me? Well, these abilities were given to us by an alien race called the Chreé. Long story Dad, but these aliens are *not* friendly, at least most of them aren't," Nicky told his dad.

Isa interrupts, "They gave us these abilities to eventually clone us. They want to replace our government and enslave humanity. Using us as the guinea pigs, they want to build an army to help them do just that."

The parents are trying to wrap their minds around what they just heard.

"What?" Nicky's dad replies stunned. "Are they after you guys now?"

Nicky answers his dad, "Well, we escaped and we can only assume they're hunting us."

"Wait, someone's approaching… I sense he is friendly," Isa says.

The stranger enters in human form and quickly transforms. "I am pleased to see your escape was successful. I am Chléony* (*clayo-knee). There are many of us who see our brethren's actions as a complete affront to our ways. Chlezéon, or Z as you refer to him, has relayed some disturbing information we were not privy to. You see we are part of the E.S.T. Organization. E.S.T. stands for the Essence Scientific and Technological Organization. We form part of a larger whole. By mandate, we should not share information with the other divisions except one."

"Divisions? What do you mean?" Isa asks.

"There is the Shelter Organization in charge of defense and internal security, the Pervade Organization which was established to infiltrate the human infrastructure, and finally there is Overwatch, who is in charge of all the divisions."

"So Mr. Macken is not your ruler?" asks Nicky.

"Mr. Macken, as you know him, is only in charge of the E.S.T. organization."

The parents, at first shocked by the alien's appearance, now can't believe what they're hearing. Isa's mother faints in her arms.

"Chlezéon has informed me that you were to be placed in suspended animation because you were no longer necessary. Overwatch is moving forward with the replication program. These

146

clones will in no way be your physical equals, but what they lack in power, they will eventually make up for in numbers. Since you were no longer necessary, security had been all but removed from the facility you were brought to."

"You mean there are others?" Isa asks.

"Yes, there are many others. I'm afraid you three have provided them with the final piece to their puzzle. Your parents should come with me."

"What do you mean?! We're not leaving you guys behind!" Nicky's dad yells.

"Mom, Dad you guys can't help us now. They will kill you without even hesitating. We have abilities now that can help us survive. Just as I've always believed in you, I ask you to believe in us now."

Nicky's dad pauses and looks down. With a lump in his throat he replies, "Okay Nicky. We will."

"But how will we know if you're okay?" Nicky's mother asks.

"I assure you Mrs. Hernandez, we will keep you abreast of their progress and condition." Chléony hands Willy a note.

"Now please come with me," Chléony tells the parents.

All the kids hug their parents one last time, and say their goodbyes.

Nicky's dad clears his throat. "I love you Nicky." Tears well up in his eyes.

"Love you too, Dad. Love you Mom."

"Oh! One more thing Chléony?" Nicky asks.

"Yes?"

"Do you know why we survived when so many others have died?" asks Nicky.

"Our processes have improved over many years of research. I would say, more importantly though, you three all shared a common trait … even your spirit would never give up."

Nicky's dad winks at him. "We never do! Good luck guys and go kick some ass!"

Chapter 38 - Six

As their parents walk out of the church, Willy reads the note Chléony had handed him. "Okay guys, it says: Go to 7737 Commerce Lane. Safe house." Along with the note, there was some cash.

"We can't be out in public for too long. We'll need a cab. Why don't we go back to Denny's and try to use the phone there," suggests Isa.

They split up and adapt, becoming almost invisible. They're careful walking back through the desert, since at a close distance they may still be sensed by a Chreé. Only Isa is able to block them telepathically from being identified.

When they finally arrive at the restaurant they call a cab. It arrives about a half hour later.

The cab drops them off at a beautiful home on Commerce Lane. The three stand outside the home on the driveway. It's a picturesque, upper-class, suburban street. Each house is two stories with pretty black lampposts, large trees, and impressively landscaped lawns.

"Wow, maybe we can keep it!" Nicky says.

"Please! I just want to be home. So how do we get in?" Isa asks. Immediately the door opens. "Strange, I don't sense anyone inside."

"Maybe it has a device that allows it to open when we're near," Willy says.

"Cool! Alien technology! Maybe it's full of alien blasters like in Halo. We can vaporize some Chreé," Nicky says.

"Oh God," Isa sighs.

They enter the house and immediately run around. They discover there are five bedrooms, there baths, and luckily for them a very nice pool and Jacuzzi.

"Nice house! Pool table! Oh and look a Jacuzzi and …"

"Xbox!" Nicky interrupts Isa. "Yes!"

"Guys we have to focus," Willy admonishes them.

"Relax! We've done plenty already," Nicky says.

"Yeah, chill," Isa says.

"We can all chill when we're safe and so are our parents," Willy scolds them.

A phone rings in the house. Willy picks it up.

"Hello, Z. Yes we're fine. What? Six are on the way. But … Okay I understand," Willy hangs up. He looks upset.

"Well what did he say?" Isa asks with a concerned look on her face.

"He said they finally cloned us. There are six of them so far. He said these clones were specifically designed to sense us from almost anywhere in the world. That should lead them straight to us. Isa can you sense them? Can you block them from finding our location?" Willy asks.

Isa closes her eyes. After a few seconds Isa says, "I sense them, but I don't think I can block all of them. I sense they're on their way," Isa says.

"If they want a fight, they'll get one!" Willy exclaims.

"We can't risk the people in the neighborhood or the safe house location. If we have no other choice, we should face them in the desert," Nicky suggests.

"Yeah, you're right. Let's go," Willy replies.

Carefully, so they're not seen, they run through the neighborhood towards a secluded desert area many miles away.

"I sense them. They're very close. Over there, I see them," Isa says. All three see clones approaching. The three are shocked by their appearance.

Six carbon copies stood before them, two of each. The clones are wearing the same coveralls the Chreé wore.

"It's like looking in a mirror," Nicky says.

"We have been asked to acquire you. Will you surrender peacefully?" Nicky's clone speaks first.

"Wow, you look like me, but you're a jackass. No we aren't coming with you," Nicky replies.

"We are required to either terminate you or capture you," one of Isa's clones states. They stare each other down for a few seconds, and without warning the clones attack simultaneously.

Nicky's clones charge into Nicky, throwing him back approximately twenty feet and knocking him on his backside.

"Ouch! Hey, I thought we were brothers!" Nicky rubs the back of his head. "Hmmm … They didn't laugh. Guess they don't have my great sense of humor."

Nicky's clones run at incredible speeds towards him. Nicky jumps ten feet over them. He manifests a tomahawk and in midair throws it towards one clone. It moves faster than a bullet instantly killing him. When Nicky lands, the second clone throws a punch to his face. He slips the punch and sweeps the clone's legs out from under him. After two punches it's over.

Isa's clones are fast but not anywhere near as fast as she is. Isa sidesteps them and jumps towards them. Her lower half transforms into that of the palomino horse. She throws a hook kick. But the clones are faster than she anticipates. They jump out of the way.

When Isa lands, one of the clones manages to kick Isa's stomach.

Isa grunts in pain. "You shouldn't have done that," Isa exclaims. She screams, "Ahhh!" and runs at top speed towards them. Running into one of them, she hurls the clone across the desert. The other Isa clone follows and positions herself just behind Isa. The clone lifts her right arm to strike Isa from behind. But before she throws her punch, Isa gives her a reverse hook kick to the head. The Isa clone falls to the ground.

One of Willy's clones gets in front of him and the other behind. They run towards him. Willy waits and leaps out of the way. The two clones collide into each other. Willy lands and then jumps towards them. In midair he manifests his fangs and claws. They are similar in appearance to those of the grey wolf he was merged with. The only difference being his fangs are infinitely more powerful. He lands on a clone knocking him down. With one quick bite, he creates a bloody gash to the clone's neck instantly killing him. Willy ducks a punch that is thrown to the back of his head. He spins his left arm back towards the second clone, slashing his neck. The second clone collapses.

It was all over in seconds.

"Everyone all right?" Willy asks.

"Yeah," Nicky replies.

"I'm okay too," Isa says. "They were definitely tougher than the Chreé."

"Yeah and that's just the first batch. Who knows if they'll get stronger," Willy says.

Nicky responds, "Or how about thousands of them. They'll be unstoppable."

"We need to stop them at the source. We need to stop the cloning," Isa says.

"Yeah, but how?" asks Nicky.

Chapter 39 - Bored

The next day they are back at the safe house. They've been sitting all morning resting and watching TV. Nicky is bored and feeling a little homesick. He starts to sing, "School time … oh yeah … oh yeah." It helps remind him of home.

"What are you doing?" Isa asks.

"What? You don't like it?"

"Shhh … guys … the phone," Willy tells them. "Hello Z, I see. Okay, I'll let them know," Willy hangs up after a brief conversation. "It seems they just wanted to know how their clones would fare against us. We are not a priority anymore. They got what they wanted from us," Willy says.

"Did he tell you where the cloning facility is?" Nicky asks Willy.

"No. I'm sure he will, just give him time," Willy replies.

"So what do we do now?" Isa asks.

"We wait," Nicky replies.

For the next week, the three fight off boredom by training, playing the X-box, swimming, and relaxing in the Jacuzzi. After a week, they are becoming a little stir crazy.

"I love the pool and training and all, but we need to get out. If Isa senses anything, you'll let us know, right?" Nicky looks at Isa, "Come on, let's go somewhere."

"No thanks. I'm staying, too risky," Willy says.

"Isa, how about you?" Nicky asks.

"Okay, I'm bored. Let's go!"

"I don't think that's a good idea," Willy warns.

"We need a break. We're going," Isa argues.

"Fine, just be careful," Willy says.

"Yes mother," Nicky sarcastically replies.

"So how do you suppose we won't be spotted moving as fast as a comet?" Nicky asks.

"Backyards, alleyways, and don't forget, only I move as fast as a comet. You're more of a, well … fat grizzly," Isa replies.

"Very funny, enjoy watching my grizzly butt cheeks from back there," Nicky laughs.

Like two streaks, they're gone jumping over fences and running through people's back yards. They pass so fast that if a resident were outside, all they would notice would be a very strong breeze.

They stop near a strip mall.

"Look. There's some stores. We have money. Now let's spend it!" Isa tells Nicky excitedly.

"Oh no! A teenage girl shopping. I want to go home now," Nicky protests.

"Be quiet. Let's go," Isa says.

For a few hours, they almost feel normal again. They eat a pizza and even catch a movie.

On their way out of the theater, Nicky tells Isa, "You know in real life, I could have kicked that superhero's arse, and …"

Isa interrupts, "You mean we; we could kick that superhero's arse."

"No, just me," Nicky says. They both laugh.

Chapter 40 - Shock

"Knock, knock. We're home!"

"Hey, why are you pasty white?" Isa asks Willy.

"It's happened," Willy replies.

"What? What's happened?" Isa asks.

"There are thousands of them. The cloning, it's starting."

"What do you mean?" Isa asks.

Willy tells them about Z's call. "Thousands of clones are now ready."

"Oh no! Already?! But how can we stop so many?" Nicky asks.

"Z told me he'd call us tomorrow with more information."

"Okay guys, so I guess we sit around and wait for his call to see what we do next," Isa responds.

Just before bed, they do some more fight training and work on their morphing.

But what they wake up to the next morning is something they never expected to see. It's all over the news. The world felt like it had stopped.

The reporter on the TV announces, "We have the latest pictures of the small contingent of aliens. Four green aliens, approximately four feet tall, appear to shake hands with the president. They have met with government officials and have promised peace. Also, they have agreed to share many of their advanced technologies. Ladies and gentlemen, we are no longer alone."

The three sit in stunned silence for what feels like hours.

"But they weren't even in their true forms. They looked like the little green aliens from a bad fifties Sci-fi film," Nicky notes.

Willy agrees. "They're all about deception; who knows what they're up to."

The ringing phone breaks the silence.

Willy answers, "Yeah Z, we just saw the news. Okay we'll be there. In the garage … yeah, okay."

"Well, what did he say?" Isa asks Willy.

"He said we'll be driven to the church. You know, I just realized we've never looked in the garage."

"But we're not sixteen yet. What if we get pulled over?" Isa asks.

"No need, this one drives itself," Willy smiles.

"Oh, so the ghost driver will get the ticket, gotcha," Isa says.

The three enter the garage.

Nicky shakes his head in disbelief and puts his hand on his forehead, "Oh no ... another black Prius."

"Don't worry, this one is friendly. Get in," says Willy.

The interior of the car is far from stock. This is an alien craft camouflaged as a Prius. The interior seems to be made out of the same Plexiglas like material they encountered before, making the car transparent when looking out. They could see all around them, as if they were floating in mid-air. Floating Chreé language and images surround the interior of the wall, just like the room they freed their parents from. Finishing off the interior are four, black, leather like captain chairs, with more floating images just above the arm rests.

"Welcome," a pleasant voice comes from the car. "Your destination has been preprogrammed. Will there be a genre of music you would like to select?"

"Rock!" Isa yells out. *Thunderstruck* begins blaring. "Nice! AC/DC." The car backs out and drives them to the church.

When they enter the church, Z is already waiting.

"Good to see you Z," Willy says.

"Likewise, my young friends," Z says. "As was shared with the three of you previously, our protocol does not allow for classified information to be shared with those outside of their own organization. As I am part of the E.S.T. organization, it is against our laws for any Chreé from Overwatch to share information with us. However, there are some brave brethren allies sympathetic to our cause within Overwatch who risk their freedom to provide us with intelligence. Yet, we did not have any forewarning that this was being planned. This contrived outing of sorts has shaken many of us, but it seems they feared exposure, specifically from you three."

"So they ousted themselves because they feared we would? It doesn't make sense. And why did they disguise their true forms? And what's their next move?" Willy asks visibly shaken.

162

"Many questions, but I am sorry, I do not know the answers. Information is now much more difficult to acquire. In time perhaps I can answer them, but the more pressing matter for now is your clones."

"So how can we possibly stop them?" Nicky asks.

"It will be the most difficult undertaking you have embarked upon thus far, but please remember why you all survived when so many did not. You never give up. I will let you know of any further changes."

With that Z, Nicky, Willy, and Isa leave the church unsure of their next move.

Chapter 41 - Destroy

They are back in the safe house. After a few hours Nicky is bored, and when Nicky's bored, his curiosity takes over.

"So, let's say they force a merge with The President. How do they make people believe he's The President? Wouldn't someone be able to tell? I mean the whole world watches The President," Nicky asks.

Willy answers, "Well, Z told me unlike us, they've mastered accessing the memories and knowledge of whoever they merge with emulating their personalities, sense of humor, and even idiosyncrasies. No one can tell it's not them, even those closest to them."

"Idiosyncrasies; they are the unique way we behave," Isa tells Nicky.

"I knew that! Anyway so … just a single touch can capture a soul? And what about us? Could they capture our souls?" Nicky asks.

"Yeah, just one touch is all they need, but they can only do it to one soul at a time. *Z doesn't think it can be done to us since we were merged with Chreé.*"

"Cool. That's a relief. Still, I don't see how we can stop them. They've been executing their plan for centuries," Nicky says.

"I don't think they expected us. We're more powerful than they imagined. I'm sure they're going to want us out of the way eventually," Isa says.

"You're right ..." Nicky agrees.

Nicky, Isa, and Willy start back with their daily routine of training, playing X-Box, swimming, and watching TV. But after a few minutes Nicky grows restless. "Okay, I'm bored."

Nicky turns on the television to catch the latest news.

The anchorman delivered the following report, "The alien visitors have stated they would study and should have a cure for cancer within months ..."

Nicky quickly turns off the TV. "We're in trouble. These guys are going to be loved."

"We need a miracle," Willy states.

The phone rings.

"Let's hope it's our miracle," Isa says.

It's the call they've been waiting for. Z finally gives them the location of the cloning facility.

Just before they get in the car, Isa tells Willy and Nicky, "I'm proud of you guys, I think we make a cool little family." They all smile.

"Now, in the words of my father, let's go kick some ass," Nicky tells them as they all high five.

The car drives them to a secluded location in the desert. Suddenly, the car begins to levitate. The exterior transforms. It looks exactly like the ship they had encountered earlier, shiny, black, and oblong.

"Okay, even I'll admit it this is pretty awesome," Willy says.

"No autopilot guys. I'm flying this thing. Remember, I'm an expert on the Xbox, I have many hours on a flight sim. This thing can't be that hard," Nicky tells his comrades.

He 'grabs' a holographic flight control wheel and flies them straight into the desert floor.

"Are we still alive?" Isa asks slowly opening her eyes.

"I think so ... nice, yeah just like the Xbox," Willy smirks.

"Hold on. I got this," Nicky tells them confidently.

"No! We'll stick with autopilot!" Willy yells in protest.

A holographic image appears in the center of the ship and shows their route.

"That looks like Russia," Isa says as she looks at the holographic image.

"Shall I navigate to the waypoint?" the ship asks.

"Yes," Willy answers.

The alien ship takes off vertically at about a forty-five degree angle. When they are just above the clouds, the speed begins to increase and suddenly the three are thrown back into their seats.

They cannot believe the unnerving silence. They expected loud rockets like the spacecraft and aircraft they know. But, the alien ship is not propelled by rockets. No human has ever traveled this fast. They are moving at twice the speed of the space shuttle.

They arrive in eastern Russia relatively close to Alaska in less than half an hour. The three see an expansive valley with green, rolling, grassy mountains and a sparkling river. The ship touches down near the river.

"That was the most intense thing ever!" Nicky yells.

"We have to do that again, but only after I throw up," Isa says holding her hand to her mouth.

"Please travel to this location." The ship interrupts them. The holographic image shows them where the entrance is. It was about ten miles northeast of their location, past the river at the bottom of a mountain.

The three step out, adapt, and cautiously race towards the facility.

They arrive a few seconds later. Like many of the things the Chreé have built, this facility is underground.

"I sense our clones. Many of them are guarding the facility. Z told me on the call that he was able to modify the cloning process without being detected. These clones should not be able to sense us like the first six," noted Isa.

"Really? When were you going to tell us this?" Willy asks Isa.

"Sorry, in all the excitement I forgot," Isa apologizes.

"Okay, well, that will give us a tactical advantage," Willy says.

"Yeah, and we'll need any advantage we can get," Nicky agrees.

They huddle behind a large rock just outside the facility.

"Careful, guys. Even when adapting to our surroundings, they may be able to make us out because of their enhanced sight," Isa warns them.

"Isa, could you sense where some of them are? Maybe we could find a way in," Willy says.

"I sense a large group; follow me." They follow Isa. "Here, just below us. It must be where they're being cloned."

"Let me give it a shot." Nicky manifests his claws and starts to dig.

"Wait. Slow down. We don't want them to hear us," Willy warns.

After a few minutes, Nicky reaches the outer wall.

"This has to be several feet of concrete. If we break in, our stealthy entrance will be compromised," Willy says.

"Wait a minute … we look just like all of them. So why not just walk in? You told us Z says he modified the cloning process so they can't sense us," Nicky suggests.

"I agree. It's worth a shot, but where's the front door?" Isa asks.

"I have an idea. We spoke about our unique abilities. You know what bears do best, besides eat? They smell. I would guess the strongest smells will come from the entrance. Just follow my nose." Although they have a sense of smell vastly superior to any earthly organism, Nicky's is far more acute because of his merger with a grizzly bear. Nicky begins sniffing for the entrance.

"Smell? This isn't going to work," Willy says skeptically.

"Trust me, my little Chuck Norris." Nicky starts walking. Nicky leads them to what he believes to be the entrance.

"This has to be it," Nicky declares.

"I doubt it," Willy responds.

They look for a way in until the surface opens and a door lifts vertically from the ground. An Isa and Willy clone walk out. The three quickly enter.

"I told you I'd find it," Nicky smirks at Willy.

"Even if their senses are nowhere as sensitive as ours, they may eventually figure out who we are," Isa states.

"Yeah, let's destroy this place and get the hell out of here, as quickly as possible," Willy declares.

They begin to casually walk down a hall.

"I see. As usual the Chreé have the best interior decorators money can buy. Can one of them not merge with Martha Stewart?" Nicky laughs. The other two don't find him as quite funny as he finds himself.

A clone of Nicky approaches the kids.

"Careful. When he smells us, he may be able to tell we're not one of them," Isa warns them.

Nicky decides to have a conversation with him. "Hey! Um ... Sorry me, I mean clone, I mean, ahh ... forget it." Nicky punches him in the jaw and knocks him out. "Ha! I just knocked myself out ... literally."

A strange deep, almost robotic, voice comes through telepathically; it's a Watcher.

"What has transpired?" The Watcher inquires in the Chreé language.**

"Our brethren was not following protocol. He was neutralized for disposal," Willy tells the Watcher in a monotone voice.**

"Acknowledged," the Watcher responds.**

"Phew! I overheard a guard say something like that once," says Willy relieved. "We have to find and take out the Watchers first. Isa, can you sense them?"

Isa closes her eyes. "Yeah, I sense them, follow me."

They try to walk inconspicuously through miles of white corridors to a small door.

"Here … we have to be fast, or they'll alert everyone," Isa warns them.

"I'll take the door. Ready, go!" exclaims Willy.

With one kick, the door explodes open. There are five startled Watchers standing inside. The three immediately take all five of them out.

"Do you sense any others?" Willy asks Isa.

"No. That's all of them."

"Now let's find where they make these things," Willy says.

Willy closes his eyes and concentrates on his enhanced hearing. He has the most sensitive of the three, a trait from the grey wolf. "The most intense sounds are coming from down this hall. Follow me."

They arrive at large double doors minutes later.

"Wow! Bigger white doors!" Nicky grins. They open the doors and are stunned.

The three kids stare at rows of thousands of clones, all of them immersed in see-through basins full of a blue, gelatinous-like substance.

"Man, this is so weird. It's like a bunch of us sleeping naked in Jell-O," Nicky observes.

"Remember guys … they'll be used to enslave us all. We have to do this!" Isa reminds them.

A clone enters the room. He is wearing what looks like a clear, plastic suit over his dark, blue coveralls. The same coveralls they are all wearing. "Why are you not in 'decam'?" he asks.

"Uh … decam? Oh yeah sorry we were just about to …"

"Order of termination for disobedience. Leave now and dispose of yourselves in the termination room."

"Yeah, okay. We'll get right on that." As Willy kicks the clone in the head, he slips on some of the blue, gelatinous liquid that leaked onto the floor from one of the basins. He just grazes him barely knocking him down.

"The traitors are here!" The clone sends this message telepathically to all of the clones near him. "Sense them brethren; they are in the birthing room."**

"Hurry!" Willy yells, but it's too late. The giant doors open and dozens of clones start pouring in.

"Oh crap!" Nicky yells. "Wow, that is a lot of sexy ... the ones that look like me anyway."

"Oh, shut up!" Isa yells.

"We have an advantage. We can telepathically link, so we can tell who's who once the fight starts. They'll be confused," Willy says.

Suddenly, a gunshot is fired. They all hear the bang. Isa is hit in the leg. She doesn't even realize it. Just like the body attacks a foreign bacteria or virus, her body almost instantaneously heals itself and dissolves the bullet.

Isa looks down, «I think I was shot! But I don't feel anything! I was shot. There's a hole in my coverall. Whatever the Chreé did to us seems to be working.»

More shots are fired, but now the three are expecting them. The three kids begin to concentrate on the warrior and animal spirits

174

that are now a part of them. Willy runs towards them slashing and biting anyone near him. Nicky starts killing any clone in his path.

After a few minutes of battling, Isa kills the last few with her bow and arrow.

«That was too easy. Hurry before more clones get here!» Isa yells. Using her manifested bow and arrow, she quickly starts destroying the alien machines around them. Her arrows travel faster than bullets.

The Plexiglas like machines around the perimeter and many of the basins are on fire, explosions erupt everywhere. Technology developed over hundreds of years is destroyed in seconds.

The double doors slide open again.

«More clones! There must be hundreds of them!» Willy shouts.

The battle is fierce, bloody, and chaotic. It is close quarter fighting. Wave after wave of clones pour in. Bodies lie everywhere in pools of blood. Sounds of screams, grunts, bone crunching, and the unmistakable and disturbing thuds of bodies impacting the walls and floor are deafening. The reverberations can be heard throughout the miles of corridors.

«There are only about ten left near the entrance!» Isa yells with as much energy as she could muster.

Nicky limps up to them. Using his sonic weapon, he growls and blows them back towards the wall. All of them fall unconscious.

An eerie silence surrounds the beaten warriors. Thousands of clones now lay motionless in this enormous room. It is a gory scene. Isa, Willy, and Nicky are bloody and badly injured. Their bodies are almost overwhelmed by all of their injuries.

"We have to get out now!" Willy yells through the pain.

They try to run out quickly, but their wounds prevent their bodies from healing as they normally would. Exhausted, they began to slowly head towards the exit.

More clones wait at the exit.

Isa sees them first. "Oh no," she sighs.

They can see and hear the blue pulses of energy exploding outside. Clones are being struck and killed.

"Where's that coming from?" Nicky asks.

The ship that had brought them there was now trying to protect them. They battle what was left of the clones to escape. Willy takes the worst of it. Finally they are able to limp over to the ship and enter it. They fly away, all badly injured, but still alive. Nicky tries to reassure Willy just before he passes out, "You'll pull through, don't worry you'll pull through buddy." Nicky yells to the vehicle, "Get us to help!"

The vehicle replies, "Chlezéon has been contacted."

"Come on Willy …" Nicky pleads. But he and Isa are so badly injured themselves, they could hardly be of any help.

Chapter 42 - Healing

"He'll make it. He has to," Isa says.

"I know he will …" But Nicky isn't really sure if he will. Nicky does something he never really does. He closes his eyes and prays.

The vehicle takes them back to the church. Z is waiting.

They limp into the church with Isa carrying Willy over her shoulder.

"Put him down here," Z motions to them. "Do not despair. His body has shut down to heal. Even with the gravest of injuries, it is possible for you three to heal. Your capacity to heal surpasses even our own," Z reassures Isa and Nicky just before he leaves the church.

It was a long, painful night in the church, but by morning all three have completely healed.

Isa is the first to wake up. "We did it!" Isa celebrates with her hands up in the air.

"Yeah, we did it," Nicky wipes his tired eyes.

The two look at Willy still lying in a pew. "Hey, I'm fine you wimps …" Willy laughs.

"Come here tough guy," Nicky motions to Willy.

The three battle-worn kids hug.

"You know, those clones were probably more powerful than any army on earth, and we beat them! At least they can't clone for a long, long time," Willy says.

"How many more do you suppose are left?" Nicky asks.

"Who knows? Thousands probably, and the Chreé are not going to be happy after what we did," Willy says.

"Yeah, but for today, let's just celebrate," Isa says.

Out of the blue, a cell phone left behind in the church rings. "Hello?" Willy answers. "Thank you, Z … what? There's another one. But we barely survived. Okay, I understand, thanks." Willy slowly hangs up.

"There's another facility!?" Nicky exclaims.

"Yeah there's another one. It's in the Arizona desert," Willy replies.

"But I thought …" Nicky starts to say.

Willy interrupts screaming, "We all thought!"

Willy and Nicky glare at each other.

"Relax guys," Isa stands in between them. "We never give up and I don't think the Apache spirits in us would let us quit anyway. Let's get in as much training as we can before we go see our sweet brothers and sisters, Okay?"

"I'm sorry," Willy apologies to Nicky.

"Don't worry about it, let's just focus on the next mission. Let's just hope it's easier than the last one."

Chapter 43 - Again

Back at the safe house, four days have passed since they received Z's last call. Stuck in the house they are growing bored of doing the same things day after day.

"Good morning boys," Isa says with a smile as she walks into the kitchen.

"Somebody forgot to buy the salmon. What am I going to eat?" Nicky says rifling through the refrigerator.

"Hey, I've got wheatgrass," Isa smiles.

"Bleh … I'll leave the wheatgrass to the horse," Nicky replies. They all laugh.

After breakfast and a long, boring day, the call they have been fretting finally comes in.

Willy answers, "Yeah, we're ready. Thanks for everything Z. We'll try our best."

"Ready guys? The vehicle is preprogrammed. Let's go," Willy tells them.

They enter the vehicle. It backs out and transforms under the cover of night and takes off.

"Z told me that three large rocks surround the entrance. When we approach, the door will open like before. They'll be expecting us, so the Watchers are on high alert. Z warned me that they've changed tactics. They can't sense us, but they can sense each other. So, if we're close enough they'll know we're not one of them," Willy says.

"Damn, this will be harder than before," Nicky says.

"Yeah, but we know what to expect now. Plus we're tougher than the first time; obviously our skills increase the more we use them, but somehow I feel more powerful now," Isa tells them.

"It's true. It's as if the more we are connecting to the spirits, it is somehow making us more powerful," Nicky says.

"I feel it too! Well, were going to need it. I'm sure the Chreé will throw everything they got at us," Willy states.

They quietly land many miles away. It is pitch dark … for normal humans anyway.

"You guys see the rocks?" Nicky asks.

"Yeah we see them," Isa replies.

They adapt and carefully begin their trek.

"You guys suppose our essence goes somewhere when we die?" Nicky asks while they travel.

"We won't find out today," Willy reassuringly responds.

"Yeah, we got each other's backs. What can go wrong?" Nicky looks at Isa and Willy, then smiles.

"Always brother," Willy says.

"And don't forget the sister, too," Isa smiles.

They arrive at the rocks. A hidden door lifts from the desert floor.

"Between my hearing, your smell, and Isa's telepathy, it should be easy to find the cloning room again," Willy tells them.

"The only problem will be getting out," Nicky says.

This facility is longer, but has the same basic layout with the obligatory white walls. Even the clones' enhanced eyes haven't spotted their adapted bodies. They search until Isa senses the cloning room.

"I think I know where it is." Isa leads them to a massive double door. Right above the door is the same glowing green light from the last facility. "This must be it," Isa says.

When the double doors open, they are amazed … again.

"Whoa! There are a lot more basins here," Nicky says looking up in disbelief.

They freeze for a second at the sheer magnitude of the room. It's similar to the last creation room, except there are thousands of basins stacked horizontally and vertically. They are stacked about fifty feet high, and each basin is dripping the gelatinous blue fluid to the basin below it. The three can only guess how many they're looking at.

"Looks like they learned how to make better use of the space," Nicky points out.

"We still haven't been spotted. We need to destroy this place as quickly as possible and get out with minimal engagements," Willy suggests.

"Yeah, like Agent 47 in *Hitman*," Nicky interrupts.

"I need you to focus, Nicky. Okay guys, first we destroy the machines around the perimeter, second those crystals above the basins, and finally the basins where the clones are created. We have to move fast and stay hidden as long as we can," Willy tells them.

The three move so fast that the human eye would have difficulty seeing anything but a blue blur. After the first explosion, the ear piercing screams of the Watchers begin.

Once all of the alien machines are destroyed, they focus their attack on several massive blue crystals situated approximately a hundred feet high above the basins. As the room fills with smoke, clones begin to enter.

«Hide!» Willy says telepathically. They start climbing the basins reaching the crystals 100 feet in the air. They adapt their bodies perfectly, blending with the crystals high above.

«Nicky, take the center rows, I'll take the left, and Isa take the right,» Willy instructs them.

They jump down and land as quietly as possible. They begin to sprint, shattering basins as they speed past, and in the process, running through clones. Destroying the bottom rows begins a chain reaction. Basins start collapsing on each other. The clones begin to attack. They cannot fight and remain adapted; they are now exposed.

Nicky begins to fight back. Several clones lay either unconscious or dead at his feet.

More begin to pour into the room.

«Isa, there are too many. I need you to focus on the clones from a distance. We'll keep at the basins!» Willy tells her.

Many of these clones are now armed with machine guns. The three can now easily see the bullets as they travel towards them. Any bullet that manages to hit one of them is quickly absorbed and any internal damage is healed instantaneously.

Isa's arrows begin taking out clones as quickly as she releases them. She moves around the room with amazing speed and agility.

«Okay, Isa, we've destroyed all the basins,» Nicky tells her.

«Go, go, go,» Willy yells. This time they try not to engage, but rather avoid and take out the clones only when necessary.

But the corridors are full of them.

Nicky roars and clears a path.

«Run through them now!» Willy yells. Willy leads the charge, his claws tearing and slashing as he runs. «I see the exit.»

They finally make it outside. «Oh no, not again!» Isa yells.

Chapter 44 - Awe

"How many do you think there are?"

"Thousands I guess," Nicky answers. They all stop and simultaneously start to concentrate on their essences. Connecting, they start to dimly glow a light blue as the essence begins to surge through them.

"You guys see that mountain?" Willy points to it. "Let's get to the top. We'll have a tactical advantage up there."

They quickly reach the top with clones following close behind. The clones start ascending. They don't know how or why, but all three feel compelled and begin making a beautiful sound, like a Native American war song. Nicky, Isa, and Willy begin glowing more brightly. Their essences are somehow making them more powerful with every passing second, almost as if preparing them for the battle ahead. The clones are almost at the top with them.

In waves of forty to fifty clones at a time, they begin to reach the peak. Isa begins flinging arrows desperately. Nicky's tomahawks and Willy's war clubs are raining down on the clones so fast, they appear only as blue streaks across the sky.

Eventually, because of their overwhelming numbers, clones begin to reach the peak and the battle turns to hand-to-hand combat. Each of the kids have now manifested their powerful animal weaponry.

The beautiful and powerful legs of the palomino horse emerge from Isa. At the same instant, the intimidating claws and teeth of the grey wolf appear as a part of Willy. Nicky manifests menacing claws and teeth like those of the grizzly bear. All of them glow more brightly and intensely as the essences that flow through them increase their power.

Isa begins to kick and strike the clones tactfully and at amazing speeds as they approach her. Her kicks look like blue streaks. They are so powerful and precise that she kills multiple clones with every kick. Dozens upon dozens of clones fly through the air with every devastating blow.

Nicky fights in a much more aggressive manner than Isa. He's delivering such vicious strikes and slashes that bloody bodies begin amassing all around him. Clones begin to fear getting near him, especially when he begins to roar. Any clone in the way of his devastating sonic weapon is instantly sent flying, eventually to the bottom of the mountain.

Willy attacks in an aggressive but tactical style. He advances with incredible agility, retreats, then slashes and bites. His speed is devastating to the clones as he slaughters them before they even have time to mount an attack.

In all of the mayhem, three clones in a prone position manage to crawl through the blood near Nicky's back. Nicky has almost lost control to his grizzly essence allowing one of the clones to stand and kick him on the side of the right knee. He falls to one knee. The other two clones grab him and quickly throw him off the mountain.

Isa can see what's happening. "Nooo!" she yells.

Willy stops and can only stare helplessly at what is transpiring.

As Nicky falls down the mountainside, he closes his eyes and thinks back to his training. He tries to connect with the eagle whose essence he shares and suddenly …

Nicky manifests wings!

"Ha! Ha … YES! I knew I could fly!" Beautiful blue, glowing eagle wings could be seen by everyone as he soars back up the mountain side. Everyone on the mountain stops fighting for just a second and stares in awe.

"He did it! He did it!" Isa screams.

"They can't stop us!" Willy yells.

Their essences begin glowing even more intensely than before. The light projected from their bodies is almost blinding. The top of the mountain glows so intensely that in can be seen for miles around. The skill and the power that the three demonstrate is power this earth has never witnessed. The battle is so intense that the topography of the mountain is permanently changed.

Finally it's over. Tens of thousands of clones lay dead all around the area.

After Nicky lands, he hugs Willy and Isa.

"Unreal! The clones never quit! They just kept coming. They really were like us," notes Isa.

Police lights can be seen in the distance. The lights are getting closer and closer. Their alien vehicle arrives.

"Take us home, buddy. Take us home," Nicky says.

Chapter 45 - Ring

Beat up, but ecstatic, all three make it home. They arrive laughing.

"That was awesome! You guys kick more butt than I thought was possible!" Nicky exclaims.

"Hey, and you flew … I couldn't believe it," Willy laughs.

"I always believed I could, and I know in time we'll all fly!"

"So," Isa asks, "What's next?"

RING!

"I wonder who that could be," Nicky says.

They all smile.

"Hello?"

We appreciate you taking the time to read ESSENCE! If you enjoyed reading it, please consider writing a review of the book or take a moment to tell a friend. Word of mouth and reviews are a self-publishing author's best friend. Your time is much appreciated.

Look for the **Pervade Org.**

coming soon!

William Fernandez lives in South Florida with his wife and four kids.
Essense is the first book that he has written. It was his life-long ambition
and desire to write a novel. For over a year, he would tell his children
stories of their special powers. One early morning, he woke up and decided
to begin writing. This novel began at 3:30 a.m. The rest is in these pages!

This book is a work of fiction. Any likeness to any real events or real people, living or dead, is purely coincidental.

Editors: Laura Fernandez and Catherine Kaplan
Proofreader: Sandra Riker
Cover Art: Brittany M. Willows

Made in the USA
Charleston, SC
12 November 2015